7/01-1
JUL 01
2/08-4

GLEN ELLYN PUBLIC LIBRARY

W9-BEC-943

Run if you Dare

AUTHOR
Randy Powell

# RUN if you dare

### RANDY POWELL

GLEN ELLYN PUBLIC LIBRARY
400 DUANE STREET
GLEN ELLYN, ILLINOIS 60137

Farrar Straus Giroux  New York

WITHDRAWN

Excerpt from *Little House on the Prairie*, text copyright 1935 by Laura
Ingalls Wilder, copyright © renewed 1963 by Roger L. MacBride. Used
by permission of HarperCollins Publishers. Please note: "Little House" ®
is a registered trademark of HarperCollins Publishers, Inc.

Copyright © 2001 by Randy Powell
All rights reserved
Distributed in Canada by Douglas & McIntyre Ltd.
Printed in the United States of America
Designed by Nancy Goldenberg
First edition, 2001
10 9 8 7 6 5 4 3 2 1

Library of Congress Cataloging-in-Publication Data
Powell, Randy.
    Run if you dare / Randy Powell.— 1st ed.
        p.  cm.
    Summary: Fourteen-year-old Gardner, trying to find some direction
    in his life, is shocked to discover that his unemployed father considers
    himself a failure.
        ISBN 0-374-39981-6
        [1. Fathers and sons—Fiction.   2. Identity—Fiction.   3. Seattle
    (Wash.)—Fiction.]   I. Title.

PZ7.P8778 Lo   2001
[Fic]—dc21

                                                                      00-57268

For Judy, Eli, and Drew, with love

RUN if you dare

Back in mid-August I bought my dad the perfect birthday present. I had it hidden in my backpack as I walked up the driveway between Dad's old Toyota Corolla and the overgrown lawn. It was my job to mow the lawn, but I couldn't bring myself to do it until someone (her name was Mom) got on me about it.

Waves of metallic heat shimmered off of the car. Early Elton John blared from Dad's boom box in the garage, where he was sitting on a yellow stool cleaning his golf club heads.

"Hey, Gardner," he said. "Just the man I wanted to see."

In the garage the air was cool and the acoustics were good. Dad was using a wire brush on the club heads. Cakes of dried dirt were scattered on newspapers spread out under him on the cement floor. He wore old tennis shoes, baggy khaki pants, a long-sleeve work shirt, and his old college baseball cap. His face was stubbled with whiskers.

"Name this tune," he said.

" 'Love Lies Bleeding.' "

Dad pointed at me. "You are good."

He liked that I knew his music from his high school and college days.

There was hardly room for two bodies in the garage, let alone two cars. That was because Dad used the garage as his personal storage room, crammed it with boxes of old LPs, CDs, cassettes, books, sports memorabilia. His magazines took up the most space. He didn't collect them, he stockpiled them. Stacks leaned every which way. He had at least one issue of probably every magazine you could think of, except for nude magazines, which he didn't bother with.

"You'll never even begin to read all those magazines in one lifetime," Mom would say.

"You got me there," Dad would say.

Back in March, when he'd first gotten laid off from his job with King County, Dad had promised that one of his home-improvement projects would be to clear out the garage.

"You don't seem to be making much progress out there," Mom had reminded him during the summer.

"It's periodical progress," he'd said. Then he winked at me to make sure I'd gotten the pun. "I just have a lot of *issues* to deal with right now, Jamie."

It got a laugh from me, at least.

Unlike Mom and my big sister, Lacy, I seemed to be the

only family member who appreciated Dad's humor. Like when he'd gotten laid off, Mom had said we should have a garage sale and maybe even sell the piano, which none of us had touched for years. Dad had said, "Oh, don't be selly." I thought that was a pretty good one.

"Love Lies Bleeding" faded out. Dad hit the stop button on his boom box.

"Guess what I bought today," he said.

"What?"

"A new driver."

"Whoa. Let's take a look."

I put down my backpack, making sure it was zipped up all the way so he couldn't see what was inside. He handed me the golf club.

"Way too expensive," he said. "But my buddy at the pro shop gave me a great deal. I know I ought to feel guilty for spending so much on a driver."

"Like you always say, 'When a man sees something he wants, he should go for it,' " I said.

"That's right," Dad said. "I'll have to use that on your mom tonight. You do some exploring today? Where'd you end up?"

"Neighborhood called Madrona."

"I know it well. Nice little golf shop there."

"Skeepbo call yet?" I asked, still examining the golf club.

"Not that I know of."

Aidan Skeepbo, my best friend since first grade, had spent the first half of the summer at a weight-reducing dude

5

ranch for rich overweight pampered youths, and the second half with his parents on a Mediterranean cruise. They were due to fly in to SeaTac from Rome sometime that afternoon.

"Feel the grip on that baby, Gardner," Dad said. "Graphite shaft. Forged titanium club head, precision tungsten screws."

"Nice balance," I said. "I bet she gives good long ball flight."

"You know it. Go ahead, take a few swings."

I carried the club out to the driveway in front of Dad's car.

"On the grass," he said. "Scrape it on the driveway, you're toast."

I took some swings, cutting swaths through the shoetop-high grass. "Awesome. Feels like you can drive the ball a mile. Heck of a purchase, Dad."

"That's what I think."

"No doubt about it," I said.

"We'll see what your mom says."

I untucked my T-shirt and started wiping the grass stains off the brand-new club head. Dad watched me for a minute. He cleared his throat.

"Not too much summer left," he said.

"No, not too much."

"It goes by fast," he said.

"Yeah, it does."

"I'd hoped we could've done a few more things together," he said. "I'm sorry . . ."

"That's okay," I said. "You've had other things to worry about."

I held the driver out to him, but he didn't take it. He looked at me like he wanted to say something more but couldn't.

"Here you go," I said. "It's a beauty."

He took it. "Thanks, pardner."

## 2

For dinner there were white raisins with little sniblets of fruit and chicken chunks and chutney in a spicy yellow curry sauce. All spread over a bed of white rice. Not bad. It sure was nice when my eighteen-year-old sister worked the early shift at Pizza Corner so she could come home and cook meals like this.

Lacy waited on my parents and me as if she were the hired cook, and she hardly ate anything herself. She said she'd been nibbling on pizza all afternoon.

"Lace, you've done it again," Dad said.

"Delicious," Mom said.

"I put in too much tarragon," Lacy said, finally sitting down with us at the kitchen table.

"It's perfect, hon," Mom said.

"Very fluffy rice," Dad said. "I'll have a bit more."

Lacy popped back up and went to the stove to serve him.

For dessert there were fresh, cold sliced peaches. Cream and sugar optional.

My sister was a perfectionist, but she did everything by the book, so it was always kind of ordinary perfection. She really had only two flaws, one minor and one major. The minor one was that she sometimes forgot to flush the toilet in the bathroom we shared, so when I lifted the lid, I would be greeted by a tequila sunrise. Her major flaw was that she saw the best in everyone, except herself.

"You got some sun today, Gardner," Mom said. "Aidan call yet?"

"Not yet."

"Those international flights," she said. "You never know what time they'll get in."

"I bought a new driver today," Dad said. He waited a few seconds, then continued. "Charged it. Cost me as much as a Buick. I probably shouldn't have."

"Oh?" Mom said.

"It was a selfish purchase," Dad said. "It's like taking food right out of the mouths of our babes. Babes, will you forgive your dad?"

"For a club of that quality, you bet we will," I said. Dad gave me a quick smile.

Lacy cut a glance at Mom and said nothing.

"It's an awesome club," I said.

"Jamie, the torque on that baby," Dad said. "Graphite shaft, titanium club head, precision tungsten screws for flawless balance. I thought I'd go hit a bucket or two of balls at the driving range tonight. I can't wait. This instrument has the engineering of a Tomahawk cruise missile."

"All for the price of an Oldsmobile," Mom said.

"Buick," Dad said.

There was silence. I ate my final peach, picked up the bowl, and drank the remaining sweet yellowy milk.

"I wonder why they call them 'buckets,'" Lacy said after a while. "They're really more like wire baskets. Why don't they say hit a 'basket' of balls."

We all helped clear the table, except for our current resident breadwinner, Mom, who sat contemplating the dusk descending on the backyard.

Dad went to her and put his hand on her shoulder.

"What's the matter, Jamie?"

"Hm?"

"I'll take it back. I shouldn't have bought it."

"That's not what I was thinking about. I was off somewhere else."

"Where? What were you thinking about?"

"Oh, something I did today."

"What did you do?"

"Canceled my subscription to the lecture series."

"You didn't."

"How do I have the time to go, Cam?"

"Cripe, it's only once a month. And it's in the evening. And it's one of your girls' club activities."

"When this ad campaign revs up, I'm going to be working

a lot of evenings. And when I'm not working, I'll be too exhausted. And it costs too much money. And besides," Mom went on, "some of those people in that audience got on my nerves. They'd ask these long-winded academic questions, obviously just to show off how much they knew. I really started to feel intellectually inferior." Mom sighed. "I guess that's my true problem. Inferiority. Life is just one big contest to impress everyone else."

"You're the smartest one in your girls' club," Dad said.

"Then how come they're all rich? They all have brand-new luxury cars and expensive jewelry and gigantic houses and housekeepers and cabins in the mountains and country club memberships. And their children all go to private schools. And take riding lessons, for God's sake. And are set up for life."

"They don't all take riding lessons," Dad said.

He kept his hand on her shoulder. Mom laid her cheek wearily against the back of his hand.

"I don't need a new driver," Dad said.

"Oh, hon, keep it. Enjoy it. At least you get pleasure from it. Go hit a bucket. Hit two."

## 3

"I don't see why he has to spend all his time and money on golf," Lacy said after Dad had left for the driving range.

Lacy was loading the dishwasher, Mom was making her lunch for tomorrow, and I was lurking in the corner, pretending to be occupied so that my sister wouldn't assign me a kitchen chore.

Lacy was right, the past few months it had seemed that Dad had gone a little bonkers on golf. When he wasn't entering local tournaments, he was practicing.

"I think your father's trying to make up for lost time," Mom said. "He's always wanted to dedicate himself to something. He'd deny it if you asked him—it would embarrass him—but he's always had this dream of being a pro golfer."

"Oh, give me a break," Lacy said.

"It's good to have a dream," Mom said. "Even at his age."

"We're going broke from him chasing his silly dream," Lacy said.

"We're not going broke. We've had to make a few adjustments, that's all."

Lacy's cheeks were flushed, her voice rising. "He's been loafing around for five months now. He's not contributing anything except for unemployment insurance, and that runs out this month. Doesn't he feel just a little uncomfortable throwing all that money into a stupid thing like golf, at his age, when he's unemployed? Good God, Mother, you don't even get benefits at your job."

"Yeah, I'd say he feels uncomfortable."

"I mean, he's about to turn forty-nine. Shouldn't he go back to work and start living in the real world?"

"You sound just like your grandmother," Mom said, one corner of her mouth going up into a smile. "Speaking of his birthday, by the way, I made a reservation for dinner Saturday night. Did you ask for that night off?"

"Yeah, I got it," Lacy said. "He doesn't deserve it, though."

"Look, we just need to cut him some slack for a while longer, Lace. Everybody needs some slack now and then."

I was glad to see Mom doing such a good job of defending Dad. My sister was like a grocery store tabloid: she overreacted and made a big deal out of everything.

Mom and Dad had made it clear to us back in February when Dad had gotten his thirty-day layoff notice: there was no cause for worry. The local economy was booming, jobs were everywhere in the Puget Sound area. Dad was going to take this opportunity to jump off the treadmill for a while, collect unemployment, read his Great Books, do projects around the house, do some soul-searching, figure out what direction he wanted to go from here.

Mom hadn't had an outside job for seventeen years, but she'd found a temporary job as an account executive for an advertising agency. That was what she had done for six years right after college, before Lacy was born.

Mom had a hard time, though, going back to that other world. The first couple months, she'd get home from work and soak in the bathtub for an hour, venting to Dad about all the waste and phoniness and office politics of the advertising world. She didn't do that anymore, though.

I didn't get the feeling we were hurting all that much for money. Mom's job paid a good hourly wage, and she was working a ton of hours per week. The trouble was, she was hired as a temporary contractor and not a direct employee of the ad agency, so she didn't get any benefits, like medical and dental coverage. And no paid vacations.

That had been the biggest bummer of all.

Back in July we'd had to cancel our annual family vacation to the beach. It was the first time in twelve years we missed our two weeks at the rented beach cabin. Mom had said we couldn't afford it this year, and she couldn't afford to take the unpaid time off.

Lacy finished loading the dishwasher. I bent down to tie

my shoe and considered scurrying under the table, but it was too late—she tossed me a damp rag and told me to wipe the table.

Rising to my feet, I graciously accepted the assignment.

I was pretty sure Dad couldn't be so deluded as to think he could actually join the senior pro golfing tour. But what if he *was* that deluded? Wasn't it better to have some far-fetched dream than none at all? I sure was looking for a dream. In fact, it seemed to be my mission.

I didn't have any dreams.

Last year during ninth grade, and during the three years of middle school before that, we must've had fifty motivational speakers come to our school during assemblies to give their personal testimony. Some of them were blind or in wheelchairs. Every one of them had the same two messages:

*1. Have a dream and follow it, whatever it is, wherever it leads you.*
*2. You can achieve your dream if you just believe in yourself and work hard and never give up.*

I believed all those motivational speakers. What's more, I believed my dad. Those had always been his messages to me.

## 4

"Things are going to be different around here when school starts," Lacy said.

She had microwaved some popcorn and brought it out in a big bowl. (She never just left it in the sack.) And as she often did in the evening, she made herself a cup of herbal tea. Mom had gone to bed, and Dad wasn't home from the driving range yet.

"Any lemonade?" I asked Lacy.

"Out in the fridge."

"I'll have a tall glass, please. With ice."

"Get it yourself, I'm not your waitress."

"Just as I thought. Things aren't going to be that different around here."

The video she'd checked out from the library hadn't been rewound, so I put it in the rewinder and closed the lid.

"Well, they are," she said.

"What things?"

"Things around here."

"I have no idea what you're talking about."

"You'd better be prepared, that's all."

"Okay, I will. Thanks."

Lacy and I sat on the couch, facing the blank TV, waiting for the video to rewind. I grabbed a handful of popcorn.

"You've had it pretty good this summer," Lacy said. "I've cooked most of the meals and done the housework. But when my school starts, I'm going to be working nights at Pizza Corner, as many hours as I can."

"Congratulations. You are obviously serious about your career in pizza." I shoved another handful of popcorn into my mouth and avoided her glare.

My sister had graduated from high school back in June. This fall she was starting at the local community college. She hoped to transfer to Western Washington University in Bellingham next year, when she had enough money saved up. Our folks had a college fund for both of us, but it wasn't enough.

"You'll have to rely on Dad for dinners," Lacy said.

"What, you won't be bringing home leftover pizza?"

"Go ahead and joke. Knowing Dad, it's going to be every man for himself in the kitchen. Either you'd better learn how to cook for yourself, or get ready for a lot of micro-waved macaroni and cheese."

"Mom would never allow me to starve."

"Mom is a little distracted, in case you haven't noticed. Plus there's all the hundreds of housekeeping chores that you've always taken for granted."

"Hundreds? Like what?"

"Like having toilet paper in the dispenser and salt in the shaker."

"No, that's where you're wrong. Not a day goes by that I don't appreciate having toilet paper within reach. Often twice a day."

"Yeah, well, one of these days you're gonna reach for it, and it won't be there."

"How did we get on this subject?" I reached for another handful of popcorn, hesitated, but grabbed it anyway. "I can endure anything as long as it's temporary. Summer's almost over, and this fall Dad'll get a job, and Mom will quit hers and come back and run the house and feed me."

The rewinder stopped and the lid popped up with a clatter, giving me a start.

"That's the plan, right?" I said. "You haven't heard anything different?"

Neither of us got up to load the video into the VCR. Lacy sat there on her side of the couch, the bowl between us, not saying anything, just holding her tea.

"The plan? I don't know what the plan is. I don't have a good feeling about it," she said, shaking her head. "Not good. I'm starting to feel like I don't know either one of them. Like they're strangers."

As my sister stared straight ahead, I took a moment to look at her thin lips, fair skin, apple cheeks. Midwestern farm-girl looks. Short stature, chubby legs. Pretty, though she'd deny it. I hadn't really looked at her for a while, and something was different about her tonight, something in her appearance, but I couldn't put my finger on what it was.

My sister was the kind of person who kept a diary and left it sitting out unlocked, because she never did anything worth hiding.

"All these bad vibes and feelings you're getting," I said. "How come I'm not getting them?"

She broke her stare. "You mean you haven't noticed anything?"

"What am I supposed to notice?"

"It figures. You're so oblivious."

"Here we go again," I said.

"Well, you are. It's amazing how everything goes right by you. You live in that filthy pigsty of a bedroom and probably don't even notice what a pigsty it is. Everything going on around you, you ignore."

"You're wrong. I notice what a filthy pigsty it is."

"You devote every bit of your attention to yourself. I envy you, Gardner, really. Ignorance is bliss."

"I'm a kid, what do you expect? Kids are supposed to be ignorant. We're not supposed to know what's going on in our parents' private lives. Our parents are supposed to take care of their own problems and stick their nose into ours. Not the other way around."

"I'll bet you haven't gotten Dad a birthday present yet," Lacy said.

"You lose that one. I bought it today."

"Go get it, I'll wrap it for you."

Not one to pass up a free wrap job, I went upstairs and got the present: two packages of three orange Titleist golf balls and a big bag of multicolored tees.

Back in the living room, we compared presents. Lacy had gotten him a briefcase, obviously expensive. When she saw my present, she smiled and shook her head.

"The irony," she said. "It's so classic."

"What irony?"

"The difference between you and me. I get him a briefcase, you get him golf balls. That says it all."

"And a bag of tees. Don't forget that," I said.

"For being a pretty bright guy, Gardner, you can sure be clueless sometimes."

"The only time I feel clueless is when I talk to you," I said.

I watched as she started her precision wrap job. Once again, I had that feeling that something was different about Lacy. It was bugging me.

"I think this birthday's especially tough on Dad," she said. "Hasn't he seemed moody to you? Vague?"

"He's just on a higher plane," I said.

"I don't know," she said. "Maybe I worry too much. I know Mom and Dad keep saying how great the economy is and everything, but from what I've been reading in the papers, and what my boss, Fritz, tells me, it's great for twenty-five- and thirty-year-olds but not for forty-nine-year-olds. I worry about him. I think he's having a midlife crisis. Do you know what I mean by that?"

"Sure. It's when a man thinks he's over the hill, so he fools around with his young secretary, and she makes him feel like a stud again. Only Dad doesn't have a secretary."

"I think he's depressed," Lacy said.

"Sure, he doesn't have a secretary to fool around with."

She ignored this. "He feels like he should be out there slaying dragons and making million-dollar deals and being a big shot. He's letting himself go, too. He's very irregular about washing and shaving, and he dresses like a bum. It's putting a lot of strain on Mom. She just goes to work, comes home, crashes. That's what I'm worried about. That we're all going off in different directions and not being a family anymore. Drifting apart. Becoming strangers to one another." She sighed, rotating the package she'd just wrapped. "Maybe he'll turn it around. I hope so."

"Maybe I should get a part-time job," I said.

"Who'd hire you?"

"Thanks for the encouragement."

"You're not even fifteen yet. You can't get a work permit until you're fifteen and a half. What do you need money for anyway?"

I shrugged. "Help out with expenses around here. Save up for a car. Chip in for our vacation next summer. I don't want to miss that again. In fact, shouldn't somebody remind Mom to reserve cabin eight? That one goes quick."

"I mentioned it to both of them the other day," Lacy said. "They just nodded their heads and gave me these glazed-over stares."

"At least they nodded," I said. "Mom'll take care of it. You know, another reason I could use some money, I was thinking—and don't laugh—I was thinking about looking into buying one of those speed-reading courses. Either that, or maybe one of those weight-lifting machines. There's this one called My-T-Gym. It's an all-performance muscle-building machine. You can buy it for twelve easy payments of only—"

"Gardner."

"What?"

"Sounds great. Go for it. Get 'em both. And then you can take us all river rafting in Costa Rica, right?"

This was an old joke between Lacy and me. Going river rafting in Costa Rica was one of the hundreds of things Dad had always talked about all of us doing as a family, some-day. Lacy and I had learned, over the years, that whenever Dad started a sentence with "someday" or "one of these days," it was the equivalent of going river rafting in Costa Rica, which meant never.

"So you think I'm like Dad? All talk and no action?"

"I think you say much and do little."

"That's a better way to put it."

"You and Dad both have a problem in the focusing and following-through departments. At least now Dad has his delusions narrowed down to one—golf. Whereas you come up with a new delusion every week, but you don't act on a single one. That's your problem."

"It is, huh?"

"Sure. You know that. You've heard it before. I inherited the common sense and dependability, but you're the one with the potential. You're smart, funny, and kind of cute, but you're wasting it because you just can't find a way to make your mark. Poor Mom."

"Poor Mom? Why poor Mom?"

"She feels guilty. You heard her tonight. She wishes she could give us more opportunities, send us to expensive summer camps and ski resorts and private schools where we can flourish and shine."

This was news to me. Then again, maybe it wasn't.

"I don't know," Lacy said. "Maybe I shouldn't say anything to disturb your blissful ignorance. Maybe it's best if you just stay your old oblivious self."

"I'm not as oblivious as you think," I said. "In fact, there's something about you that's been bugging me, and I think I finally figured out what it is. Your hair. You changed your hair color!"

"What?"

"You did, didn't you. You dyed it. It's darker and a little more . . . reddish."

"Are you serious?"

"Well . . . yeah. I mean, it looks—it looks good."

"Well, Gardner, how sweet of you. You just noticed?"

"Yeah. No, actually, I, uh, think I might have noticed a couple of days ago."

"Oh, I see," she said, nodding. "Well, that's interesting, considering I dyed it last May."

She got up and put in the video, but I decided to skip it and headed up to my room.

## 5

Walking around in my room was hazardous. Piles of library books covered the floor. My only chair was buried in dirty clothes. I had to step between the gaps in the books; one wrong step, and I'd topple a stack, making for even fewer places to plant a foot.

It was getting out of control.

Mom seemed to have suspended cleaning my room for me.

I made a series of precise hops, skips, and jumps over to my bed and fell on it. My peninsula, my pier, my spit. Taking another hard sobering look at my room, I saw chaos. Lack of completion. Lack of discipline. My room was a reflection of my life.

If a stranger were to view my room and see all these books, they might deduce that I was a serious readaholic.

The problem was, I never got around to reading any of them. I'd read a few pages and actually be very interested. But then I'd put the book aside and say to myself, "Well, that's very interesting. I'll have to come back to that later and really read it carefully." But I would never come back to it. Or when I did, it wouldn't seem as interesting, so I'd pick up another and do the same thing.

But imagine being able to speed-read a whole book in one sitting.

I sat on my bed, contemplating my room.

Was it a pigsty, or a sign of eccentric genius?

I knew I was probably not an eccentric genius. All right then, suppose I was just an average kid, one of the masses. Did that mean I would never rise to great heights? Or did it mean I'd just have to work my butt off that much harder? But work my butt off at what? Was I supposed to choose something, or wait for something to choose me?

Dad's advice to me had always been that I should just let things work out for themselves. Dad thought that God played a big part in a person's life, that God had a plan for each one of us, and that His plan would unfold according to His own schedule.

Mom, on the other hand, didn't put much store in God. She preferred to stay clear of the subject.

All these books, scattered across the floor. I wanted to read every one of them. A book a day. A thousand pages a week. I wanted to collect books, have my own library, my own hoard.

All talk and no action.

River rafting in Costa Rica.

It hit me.

What all those piles of unread books on the floor reminded me of.

My dad's stacks of magazines in the garage.

It gave me a creepy feeling. As if I had inherited some weird gene from my dad.

In some ways, being a chip off the old block was scary.

**6**

Skeepbo called early the next morning and told me to come on over, so I hiked up to his house at the top of Briarcrest Hills. The houses up there in the thick cool woods are huge and private, with awesome views of Lake Washington below.

I hadn't been to Skeepbo's all summer, and it was good to be back. The place was like my second home. His parents greeted me like a long-lost son. I asked them about their trip and brought them up to date on how my family was doing. Then Skeepbo collected his beach stuff, which included the extra swim mask that I always used, and loaded it into his backpack, and we took the fifteen-minute walk to the beach club. It was at the north end of Lake Washington, in the heart of the affluent Briarcrest Beach neighborhood—not to be confused with the even more affluent Briarcrest Hills.

We'd been coming to the beach club every summer for as long as we'd been best friends. He was a member; I was his guest. The cost of membership was so beyond my parents' means, it wasn't even funny.

There were two main groups at the beach club: poolsiders and lakesiders. Skeepbo and I were poolsiders mainly because the girls' swimsuits were skimpier by the pool than by the lake, and there were fewer mothers and nannies with sand-pail-toting kids. It was also closer to the concession stand, where we bought pepperoni sticks. The spiciness of the pepperoni sticks made us crave chocolate, the chocolate made us thirsty for cold drinks, and the drinks made us crave spicy pepperoni. So we had a nice little triangle going there.

The beautiful people started showing up, anointing their bodies with suntan lotion.

"How much weight did you lose?" I asked Skeepbo.

"Only seventeen pounds."

"Seventeen pounds isn't bad."

"You think so?"

"You look like you lost more than seventeen," I said.

"No kidding?"

"Man, you look lighter."

That was pretty much all we said about his weight. It wasn't something we talked about that much, not because we were uncomfortable with it but because he had been fat ever since I'd known him. Back when I met Skeepbo in first grade, it had never occurred to me that he was fat or skinny or anything else. He was just a guy with the same weird imagination and sense of humor as me.

For instance, one of the first things we did when we became friends was invent our own elaborate system of martial arts. We called it Skeep-kwon-bo.

Over the years, he'd taken a lot of teasing and tormenting, kids at school calling him "Ski Boat," "Scab Butt," "Skid Butt," and "Real Estate." I'd always thought he was thick-skinned and wasn't bothered by all the fat jokes. That's why I was surprised last spring when he finally gave in to his parents, after three years of pressure, and agreed to go to the fat-farm dude ranch in Eastern Washington.

Skeepbo handed me some pictures he'd taken on the cruise ship of nude sunbathers on the French Riviera. I examined them. Sure enough, there were nude people. The shots were all tilted and out of focus because he'd been so busy trying to make it look like he was taking pictures of the scenery instead of the sunbathers.

He also had pictures of the people he'd become friends with at the fat farm.

"They look like a nice bunch," I said.

"Yeah, a lot of them were pretty screwed up. But nothing compared to the girls in the East Quarters."

"Who were the girls in the East Quarters?"

"The Bulmies. Bulimics. They were all gorgeous and skinny—they just thought they were overweight."

"Like mental patients or something," I said.

"Yeah. We were all mental patients," Skeepbo said. "We

spent a lot of time in therapy, trying to figure out why we abuse food so much. Learning how to get our mind off our body. We did dream interpretation, meditation, stress management. My dad, man, he freaked out. He thought it would be more like boot camp."

I laughed. "I guess it's like my dad says. We're ninety-five percent mental and five percent physical. But we end up spending ninety-five percent of our time on the physical, and five percent on the mental, when it should be the other way around."

"Well, it was definitely the other way around for us," Skeepbo said. "But we got plenty of exercise, too. Games, sports, useless arts and crafts, ballroom dancing. I tangoed and waltzed with the chubby daughters of multimillionaires."

"You have any romances?"

Skeepbo snorted and shook his head.

"How about on the cruise ship?" I asked. "You meet any Greek princesses?"

"Fell in love with many, met none."

Skeepbo had what you'd call a shock of hair that was always falling down the right side of his face so that he could scrape it back up on his head with his fingers. It was wavy and thick, professionally styled every three weeks, but usually kind of oily looking.

"All that therapy," I said. "You come away with any great realizations?"

"I realized my parents are kinder to Snoopikins than they are to me."

"It's easier to be kind to a dog than a kid," I said.

"And I realized something else," he said. "A major break-through."

"What?"

He held up his pepperoni stick. "I like to eat, and I hate to exercise."

"We ought to at least try some running," I said. "Go for a jog on the Burke-Gilman Trail."

"Jogging," Skeepbo said. "Joggers get on my nerves. I hate it when girls stick their ponytails out the back of their baseball caps."

We put on our sunglasses and took off our T-shirts and soaked up the sun and enjoyed the view. Pretty soon we got out the magnetic chessboard and started a game of chess. He was black and I was white, which was appropriate, as he had a deep Mediterranean tan and I was pale, except for my arms, which made me look as though I'd been reaching into a vat of cocoa butter.

I felt like a scrawny wimp. I really should have done some running or weight lifting over the summer, got myself bulked up. I didn't want to sit around all day mulling on the paltriness of my own torso, but when you're at the beach on a summer day, it's hard to stay up there on the spiritual plane, caring about how many books you want to read.

Just then a girl wandered in front of Skeepbo and me and gave us a glance. She was maybe a fifth or sixth grader. The girl turned her back to us and faced the pool, preparing to dive in. She had a constellation of mosquito bites on her left calf. I found this arousing. Especially from the standpoint of the mosquito.

Splash. Drops of water hit us.

Returning my attention to the chessboard, I moved my bishop and captured Skeepbo's pawn. "Check," I said. He groaned. He was rusty. Two moves later, he resigned. He sulked. He had never been a gracious loser. I tried not to gloat. He dug a paperback from the backpack and started reading, while I stretched out in the sun, feeling happy, sleepy, dopey, and at least a couple other Seven Dwarfs.

After a while, we put on our swim masks and dove to the bottom of the pool. One of our favorite pool pastimes was to ogle girls' bodies. Safe and hidden behind our masks, holding our breath on the pool bottom, we could feast our eyes from exciting and daring angles usually forbidden to boys' eyes on dry land. The wickedness of it made it more fun.

Back on dry land, we did our ogling from behind our sunglasses.

Over on the grass field were three girls from our class, all wearing skimpy bathing suits. Tippy Yamashita, Starr Woodall, and the Aztecan Beauty. Brunette, redhead, brunette. They were talking to three obnoxious guys, also in our class, who were tossing a football around and acting like they owned the beach club.

I must have been staring at them, because Skeepbo elbowed me and said, "Your drool is glinting in the sun."

"The Aztecan Beauty is wearing one of those one-piece Speedos," I said. "On the right body, those things are sexier than a bikini."

"I wish she were wearing a one-piece Skeepbo," he said.

The three guys—T.T., Janesco, and Gregerson—had their shirts off, showing off their muscles. Tyler Gregerson's skin was the same color as the football. He exuded total confidence and cockiness. He lived about a mile from here, waterfront house, and parked his ski boat at the dock, which was okay for members to do.

Skeepbo went off to see if they'd posted the sign-up sheets for the annual Labor Day weekend badminton doubles tournament. We'd won it three years in a row. We were awesome.

He was gone a long time. When he returned, he was eating another pepperoni stick, and he had a sly grin on his face.

"I signed us up," he said. "Quite a few entering this year."

"We'll own it," I said.

He still had that sly look.

"I ran into Sophie Beam at the concession stand," he said.

"Yeah?"

"She was with somebody."

"Who?"

"Somebody we haven't seen for a long time. Somebody who moved away after fifth grade."

"Who?"

"Annie Harris."

"No kidding? What's she doing here? Did you talk to her?"

Skeepbo nodded. "She and her mom moved back into their old house. I guess they never sold it, they just sublet it. She's been hanging out here all summer with Sophie. She told me to say hi to you."

"Yeah?"

"And give you a big kiss, too. Right on the lips. Are you ready?"

"No, let me lubricate them a little," I said.

Skeepbo sat down and took another bite of his pepperoni stick.

"She's filled out," he said.

"Who has?"

"Annie."

"What do you mean filled out? Fat?"

He shook his head. "You know how you said a one-piecer on the right person is sexier than a bikini? Well, she's the right person."

"Annie?"

He nodded.

"Where are they?"

"Down at the lake. Far end, almost by the hedge."

"Maybe I'll go say hello." I stood up. "Want to come with me?"

"Nah, I'll stay here. I already talked to her."

I put on my shirt and started down to the lake.

7

The day was gorgeous. Mount Rainier was stark white against the deep blue sky. The sun-dazzled lake was choppy with ski boats towing water-skiers and yee-hawing Jet Skiers doing figure eights.

I reached the shoreline and waded in. I looked around and saw Annie. I recognized her instantly, sitting next to Sophie Beam, who was plain and homely with squirrelly cheeks but a nice girl. Sophie was wearing sunglasses and reading a magazine and eating an ice cream bar. Annie was not wearing sunglasses, just sitting there on the sand with her knees up, sipping a drink through a straw, looking off in another direction, her long blond hair exactly as I had re-membered it.

I waded a bit farther out into the lake, until the bottom of my T-shirt got wet. I didn't want to take my shirt off. I felt too self-conscious about standing before a girl with my nipples exposed.

A wave came, and the cold water lapped my nuts and made me gasp and lose my breath.

When I half-turned to look at her again, I saw that she had spotted me and gotten up and was coming my way, smiling. She had filled out all right, no doubt about it.

"Hey, Gardner," she called. "Remember me?"

She waded into the lake and stopped just up to her calves, which put her a comfortable ten feet from me. At that end of the beach, we were pretty much alone.

"Sure," I said. I had always liked Annie Harris. She used to sit in front of me in fifth grade and laugh at my jokes. She was a good audience. I'd be doing something like drawing X's and O's on my desk with a pencil, designing football plays and offensive and defensive formations; she'd turn around and ask me who was winning the football game; I'd spit on my finger and rub it on the desk, smearing the pencil marks and saying in a football commentator voice, "It's a muddy field out there today, folks! A muddy field!" Things like that would crack her up.

"Turn and face that way, so I can see the back of your head," I said.

"What?" She looked puzzled but obeyed.

"That's the view I had every day for five months in Ms. Treadwell's class."

She laughed and turned back to face me. "No, I spent more time turned around talking to you. Ms. Treadwell was always saying, 'Annie, face front!' It's amazing she never split us up."

"Fifth grade," I said, shaking my head.

"Good old Ms. Treadwell," she said.

"So," I said, "you moved back?"

"Yeah, same old house and everything."

"Just up the street, right?" I said. "Have you and Sophie kept in touch all this time?"

"Yeah, she's kept me up on all the gossip. I always asked her about you."

"Oh, lotta gossip there," I said.

"Are you getting cold standing here in the lake?" she asked.

"Yes, there's a breeze," I said, feeling like a very bad actor saying very bad lines. "Let's go sit down."

Sophie had disappeared. Annie and I plunked ourselves on the grass, not far from where their blanket and stuff were. We sat with our legs outstretched, arms behind us for support. The grass was warm and tickly. A breeze came from the lake and from the direction of Mount Rainier, sometimes fresh, sometimes carrying diesel fumes from outboard motors.

"Where've you been?" I asked. "How come you moved back?"

She told me a fairly long story that I didn't quite follow. Something to do with living in New York, then San Francisco, then her dad running off with another woman. And now she and her mom were back.

"Sorry to hear that," I said. "I mean, about your dad."

"Yeah, well, it's a bummer, thanks. He lives in about five different cities and travels all the time. I think he's got a girl-friend in every port—or maybe by now he's narrowed it down to just two or three. Girlfriends."

"What is he, a salesman?"

"He's a pirate."

"A what?"

"A pirate. He fries pranes."

I laughed. "I'd forgotten how weird you can be."

"He owns his own private charter jet. He takes rich people wherever they want to go whenever they want to go there. He's always flying fashion models to exotic locations for their photo shoots. The fashion models find him irre-sistible. The bum. How about you? You still have your old traditional nuclear family and big sister and all that?"

"Still intact," I said.

"Oh, we got a cat," Annie said. "I installed a cat door for him all on my own."

"That's exciting."

"It is for the cat. What've you been doing this summer?"

"Nothing as exciting as installing a cat door."

"How's your dad?"

This took me by surprise. "My dad? He's fine. Why?"

"You used to talk about your dad. You'd talk about stuff you did together. You used to go drive around and play chess or something."

"I'm surprised you remember that," I said.

"I thought that was so cool, how you were like best friends. When I moved away, I used to think about that. I wondered if you'd still be that way. Are you?"

"I guess so," I said. "Although my dad is kind of like yours."

Annie looked puzzled. "A bum?"

I shook my head. "You said your dad's a pilot. Mine's been up in the air, too. On a different plane."

I hadn't thought about saying it or planned to say it, the words just came out of me.

"We did go camping once this summer," I said after a minute, "up by Deer Lake. We parked at the trailhead and rode our mountain bikes a few miles up and then hid the bikes in some bushes and hiked three miles to Deer Lake and camped there. It was awful. They were doing helicopter logging a few miles away, so there were these noisy choppers going back and forth the whole time. A species of wood gnat decided to die in my ear canal. When we got home, I had to go to the doctor and have my ear dredged. I have no idea why I'm telling you this."

Annie was laughing. "Gnat's another story," she said.

We sat for a while, looking out at the lake. The breeze came, and for a moment I caught from Annie a familiar smell of fresh soap that I used to smell when she sat in front of me.

"Remember when we used to go to the custodian's office to clean the erasers?" she said.

"The old motorized eraser cleaner," I said.

"And that song we made up, 'Chalk Dust Flying up Your Nose.' "

"Yeah."

"And the Chair Squad. Remember that? We were co-captains of the Chair Squad. And of course, your crowning achievement, you were emcee of the fifth-grade talent show."

"Yeah." I squinted out at the lake.

"Yeah," she said. "Boy. What a year."

She had just named all my greatest achievements. Not just my achievements up to fifth grade, but up to right now.

"Oh, there's Sophie," Annie said. "She's signaling to me."

I looked to where Annie was looking. Over on the dock, where the boats were tied up, Sophie was waving. Standing next to Gregerson, T.T., Janesco, and the Big Three—Tippy, Starr, and the Aztecan Beauty—along with about a half dozen others, Sophie was signaling for Annie to come over and join them.

"Tyler's been promising to take us water-skiing," Annie said.

She stood up and brushed the grass blades from her calves. Her bathing suit traveled right up her hips. I stood up, too, not wanting to be looking up at her body from a sitting angle. At least not without my swim mask on.

"Well, I'll be seeing you around," she said.

She turned and started off at an easy jog toward the dock. I watched her. She ran like an athlete, and that was something I didn't remember about her. She joined up with Sophie and the others, and they all distributed themselves into two boats, Gregerson's and some other guy's, a junior or senior, I thought.

I headed back up to the pool and found Skeepbo reading and eating.

"How was it?" he said.

"All right. She and Sophie went off with Gregerson and his bunch."

"Figures."

We decided to call it a day. Skeepbo had jet lag and wanted to go home to bed. Neither one of us wanted to look at another pepperoni stick for a long time.

At the intersection of Mall Way, Skeepbo and I split up. He gave me a behind-the-back wave as he trudged off toward Briarcrest Hills, carrying the backpack. I stood watching those big fat tanned legs and calves, on down to the handmade Greek sandals that he'd bought on some Greek island. I thought how good it was to have him back. I'd missed him. I should have told him that.

I turned and headed for the library.

8

For as long as I can remember, I've been going to the county branch library located on the lower level of Briarcrest Village Mall, between the ballet studio and the shoe repair shop.

At three o'clock on a hot Thursday in August, the mall was dead. It was not the place for serious back-to-school shoppers. It had three floors of specialty shops that sold nothing but one item each—cowboy hats, jigsaw puzzles, handmade children's bunk beds, bathroom accessories, oil paintings of beachscapes by local artist Vern Miller.

There'd been a rumor going around for a couple of years that a Barnes and Noble with its own Starbucks was coming, and that the whole village would be revamped and updated, and that they'd do something horrible like stick a food court on the lower level and bring in a Nordstrom and a Sears. But that catastrophe hadn't happened yet. I liked the mall exactly the way it was, dead and quiet—more like a museum or a sleepy small-town street front than a shopping mall.

The prevailing smells were the waxed wooden floors, Jake the Candymaker on the upper level, Steubens gourmet coffee shop, and Ye Olde Village Bread Co. on the main level.

As I entered the air-conditioned library, I stopped and inhaled: ah, books. When Ching, the summer student volunteer, spotted me, she waved me over to the checkout desk and reached down behind the counter and brought up a stack of books with a hold marker. "These have been waiting for you for a few days, Gardner."

I nodded and handed her my library card.

While I watched her scan each of the new books under the bar coder, I could hardly even remember placing a hold on some of them. There was a book on sailing; a book on running; an autobiography by Rafer Johnson, the decathlon star; an unauthorized biography of Tom Selleck; a book on weight lifting; and assorted novels.

"Would you like a sack?" Ching asked.

"Thanks."

I had to give Ching credit. Not once during the summer had she commented on my selections or asked if I actually read any of them. Check 'em in, check 'em out, that was Ching. Just like the pharmacists over at Pik 'n' Chooz, who never made comments on my purchases there, such as "Ah, trying a new brand of pimple medication, are we?" There's something to say for professionalism.

I left the bagged books in a nearby study carrel and sat down at one of the three side-by-side computer terminals.

Fingertips poised at the keyboard, I paused to look around. Only a couple of patrons were there: an old geezer reading a newspaper, and a mother reading a picture book to her young geezer. Jezebel, the fluffy cat who owned the entire library, was curled up asleep in her reserved chair.

On the computer screen I selected the magazine and newspaper database and, at the computer's prompt, typed in my library number and PIN.

"Haven't seen you for a while." The head librarian, Ms. Patterson, dressed as usual like a Nordstrom sales clerk, sat down next to me. "Hey, you've been getting some sun."

Such a mom thing to say.

"Read any good books lately?" I asked.

"A few. How about yourself?"

"Well, no, not really."

She knew about my problem of checking out books and not reading them. I had told her about it long ago. She didn't seem to think it much of a problem. "There's no law that says you have to read the books you check out," she'd said.

"Looking for anything particular today or just browsing?" she asked.

"I thought I'd do a search on some of those speed-reading courses I've been seeing on infomercials," I said. "I saw one the other day. It guaranteed to teach you to read twenty times faster than your normal rate. You can read the King

James Bible in the morning and the collected works of Shakespeare in the afternoon. I'd say that would be a productive day's reading."

"I'd agree."

"Also, I thought I'd look into this thing called the My-T-Gym. You ever heard of it? It's this amazing muscle-building machine. Only twelve low monthly payments. Guarantees to enlarge and enhance the twelve muscle groups in just three weeks or your money back. The next best thing to steroids."

Ms. Patterson wished me luck and went off to help the old guy with the photocopier. I always enjoyed talking to her. She was the only authority figure I knew who never felt she had to offer me advice. Ms. Pasco, the other librarian, always wanted to give me novels about teenagers who think they're failures and end up learning how special they are.

I spent a while fiddling around on the computer, reading some on-line articles about speed-reading courses and weight-lifting contraptions, but mostly just sitting there with my mind drifting. I thought about that meeting I'd had with Annie at the beach. She was another person I enjoyed talking to. I wondered if I'd changed much in her eyes since fifth grade, and if I'd changed for the better or worse. In fifth grade it must have seemed like I was going places. Emcee of the talent show, cocaptain of the Chair Squad. No telling where I'd be by tenth grade. Well, Annie knew by now, or she'd know soon enough: I was going nowhere.

## 9

Saturday evening before we left for the restaurant, Dad opened his birthday presents in the living room. He loved the golf balls and tees, of course. "You can never have enough golf balls," he said. "Or tees." He acted pleased with the briefcase from Lacy but cracked jokes such as "Is this for carrying my golfing scorecards, Lace? How am I supposed to fit my clubs in here?"

Then he opened Mom's present. Mom chewed her lip and picked at her thumbnail as Dad tore off the wrapper. It was a book of poems by a poet named Rilke. As he held it up, his face changed. This was no acting job—he seemed genuinely moved. Evidently, Dad and this book were old long-lost friends; he'd first met it in college but had lost touch with it and had been looking for it for a long time. It had the original German on the left side of the page, with the English translation on the right side.

Dad went over to Mom and took her in his arms, and they kissed. Lacy and I exchanged a look: *All right, Mom.*

The French restaurant where Mom had made the reservation was in an alley near Pike Place Market. It didn't have any windows. You had to figure a place with no view would have to make up for it by serving extra-good food.

Dad ordered a bottle of local wine for him and Mom; Lacy and I had sparkling cider in wineglasses. The waiter opened the wine at the table, and Dad made a show of his wine-tasting technique before giving it his okay. It was good to see Dad being his old self, the one I hadn't seen much of lately.

After the waiter left, Dad raised his glass and said, "Here we all are. What shall we drink to?"

"To the coming school year," Lacy said.

"That's a boring toast," I said.

"All right then," Lacy said. "To us. To the Dickinsons."

Mom raised her glass. "To the Dickinsons. Long may you run."

We all chinged our glasses together and took a drink.

Lacy kept her glass up. "When they give us our own TV sitcom, I think they should call it *Here Come the Dickinsons.*"

"Works for me," I said, then killed off the rest of my cider.

"You three," Dad said, "you three are the greatest thing in my life. Thanks for putting up with me these past weeks.

The time has come for me to get off my rear end and go back to work."

Mom was smiling at Dad.

"Do you kids have any idea," Dad went on, "how many jobs I had during the six years from the time I married your mom to when I was hired at King County? Anybody care to venture a guess?"

"Fourteen," Lacy and I said together.

"I had fourteen jobs," Dad said. "But finally I settled down and talked your mother into getting out of that lousy advertising business. And we went on and had two beautiful, brilliant children. Who died, unfortunately; so we had to adopt you two instead."

We all groaned and rolled our eyes. Dad must have used that one a hundred times.

Dad had brought along the poetry book Mom had given him, and now he picked it up and thumbed to a poem he seemed to know. He cleared his throat and started reading the poem in German. He didn't even pause when the waiter came and brought bread. The waiter glanced at Dad before retreating through the swinging door, probably to inform the kitchen crew that there was a guy drinking Washington wine and reading German poetry in a French restaurant in Seattle. I half-expected to see a dishwasher or cook poke his head out to have a look for himself.

One thing I had always admired about Dad was his lack of self-consciousness in public places. He just didn't give a rip what other people thought.

Dad finished the German and turned to the English version of the same poem on the opposite page. As I listened to his low, resonant voice and the words and the silences in between the words, I thought of how my dad always seemed to believe that things would work themselves out in their own way. He never seemed to worry about the outcome of things. And I thought I could do a lot worse than take after my dad. A lot worse.

During dessert Dad turned to me and said, "How about we do something tomorrow we haven't done for a long time? We'll take the chessboard, hop in the car, and drive out into the country and play a five-game tournament." I said I thought that sounded good.

In the morning I woke up at about seven o'clock and saw out my window that it was raining lightly. When I went downstairs, Dad was at the kitchen table drinking coffee and reading that Rilke book.

"Good morning," he said. "Ready to go?"

"You don't mind the rain, do you?" I said.

"Of course not. Go get the chessboard. The big one."

We had a nice chessboard with black and white squares and good weighted chess pieces with green felt bottoms, the kings about four and a half inches tall. The board folded in half so you could carry it like a briefcase and put the pieces inside it. You didn't throw them in—each piece fit perfectly in its own green felt inlay, and when you opened the board up, you could not even see the crack where it folded.

Dad brought a thermos of coffee with him, and we got into his Toyota. It was very messy. The floor and seats were littered with books, magazines, old golf scorecards, gas station receipts, dried orange peels, an old sweatshirt and golf sweater, empty Coke cans, Styrofoam cups, and even some old beer bottles.

We drove north on I-5 in the light rain with no destination, or at least none that Dad mentioned to me. We talked about general things, nothing much in particular, and after a while he asked if I was hungry. I said I was, but I could wait.

We drove another half hour, Dad drinking his coffee, and we turned off at Marysville and took a road that went northeast by the small town of Granite Falls, and Dad pulled off at a café that had a semi parked to the side and an RV and some pickup trucks in front. Dad said we'd eaten there before on a fishing trip, and I vaguely remembered it.

We went in and sat down at a booth, and the waitress came and asked Dad if he wanted coffee, and I was surprised that he said yes, considering he'd been drinking it practically nonstop all morning. I looked at the breakfast section on the back of the menu, and I was so hungry I ordered the Lumberjack Special.

A couple of booths away from us, three men with beards and baseball caps were talking quietly and looked like fishermen. In another booth was an old retired couple who wore matching windbreakers; they must have belonged to the RV. There was a younger man with a crew cut and long sideburns, sitting at the counter smoking a cigarette and drinking coffee and reading a Sunday newspaper. Dad saw me looking at the man and leaned across the table and said in a low voice, "I'll bet you anything he's the one driving that big rig out there."

We ate and watched the people come and go. I ate slowly. I wanted to savor every single bite. Dad went to use the bathroom. While he was gone, the waitress came over and poured me another glass of orange juice from a pitcher without my even having to ask, and she said in a friendly voice, "How you doing, you getting enough to eat?" and I told her I was.

When we finished we headed back out on the road, driving through Granite Falls on Highway 92 and continuing east. Dad pulled over to the side of the road because he had to pee again, all that coffee. He went behind some trees. There were no other cars.

While he was gone, I reached into the backseat and picked up one of his old sweatshirts and took a whiff of it, just to see if it would smell like my dad, and it did. I knew it was a strange thing for me to do, and I didn't know why I had done it.

We drove for another five miles until we turned off onto a small road that ran along the south fork of the Stillaguamish River. We took that for a mile or so, then pulled over next to an old picnic shelter.

"We went fishing here once, remember?" Dad said.

"I think so," I said.

The place was deserted. We got out and started game

number one of our chess tournament under the picnic shelter in the fresh forest air, with no sounds anywhere except the river. I was white and dad was black. Dad took a long time to make each move. If we'd been using a clock, he'd have run out of time.

"You've been studying your openings," Dad said.

"A little," I said.

"Mm-hm," Dad said. He sat up, concentrating. "Well, I can tell you right now I'm not going to be allowing you any take-backs."

"You haven't allowed me take-backs for a long time."

"Mm. Yes. Well, this game doesn't appear to be salvageable, does it."

"I don't think so," I said.

Unbelievably, just like that, I had won the first game. We changed sides and started game number two. Dad took even longer to make a move.

Sometimes while he pondered the board, I'd get up and walk around to stretch my legs. One of those times I walked down a trail, and a muskrat or something scuttled right across my path and just about startled me out of my pants. That second game was pretty even, and then Dad made a puzzling move, sacrificing a pawn for no apparent benefit. At first I thought it was a trap, a ploy to bait me, but after a moment's study, I concluded it was not a trap at all but a fatal blunder on Dad's part. Five moves later, I'd forced his queen into a hopeless position, and he tipped over his king, showing that he resigned. I was up 2–0.

Between games we did some exploring down by the river. I showed Dad where I had seen that muskrat or varmint or whatever it was.

"You've played two steady games," Dad said. "That second game, I kept waiting for you to make a weak move, but you didn't. I won't underestimate you again."

"You'd better not," I said.

We changed sides of the picnic table for our third game and played to a draw, which made the score 2½ to ½, my favor.

It was getting dark. We drove to a café in the town of Concrete and brought the chessboard inside and played our fourth game there while eating hamburgers and fries.

Two old men stood by and watched, discussing our moves in low mutters. After forty moves, I was up a bishop and a pawn, but Dad hung in there, hoping I'd make some late blunder. But I didn't, and I mated the black king. That made the score 3½ to ½. There was no point in playing game five.

"I can't believe it," I said. "You must be rusty."

"You have finally dethroned your old man," Dad said. "The day after his forty-ninth birthday, no less. Congratulations."

He held out his hand, and I shook it.

"It's a changing of the guard," he said. "A changing of the Gardner, you might say."

"You'll crush me next time," I said.

"I don't know," Dad said, rubbing his chin. "Your game

has matured. I remember the first time I truly, soundly beat my father, I was nineteen, and it was like crossing over into new territory. There was no turning back. From that point on I beat him regularly. You know what my dad said when I beat him that first time?"

"What?"

" 'There's another nail in the coffin.' "


We sat in the smoke-filled café, and I ordered a piece of apple pie and a glass of milk. Dad ordered a beer.

"You looking forward to school starting this year?" he asked.

"Yeah, I guess so."

"You going to do anything exciting? Try out for any teams?"

"I don't know," I said. "Maybe."

"How about the chess team? Maybe you and Aidan could do that."

"I think it's a club, not a team," I said. "Yeah, that's a possibility, I guess, although Aidan'll be busy with music. I kind of wish I'd gotten more done this summer."

"Like what?"

"Lift weights or do some running."

Dad nodded. "That would've been good for you."

"I should have got off my butt sooner," I said.

He gave a short laugh. "Ah, the voice of regret."

"I guess that's what losers say, isn't it," I said.

"I guess it is," Dad said.

"But it's not too late to get started, right?" I said.

"No," Dad said. "No, of course it isn't."

The waitress brought my apple pie and milk and Dad's beer. We ate and drank for a while without talking.

Dad said, "I always regretted I didn't do more serious running when I was your age."

"Really?"

"Or something like the pole vault or long jump. Something where you don't necessarily have to compete against another person. You can compete against yourself. Something you can measure with a stopwatch or a tape, you know? Something measurable."

"I know what you mean," I said. "Golf is like that, isn't it?"

"I suppose so. But running or jumping is much simpler. It's purer. I really regret not having specialized in something." He drank some more of his beer. "Having a specialty would have made a difference. But I was more of a dabbler."

I wanted to ask him what difference it would have made—having a specialty. It seemed important. But instead, I thought about what Lacy had said the other night, all that stuff about Dad being in some kind of a midlife crisis. He seemed to be in a fairly good mood considering he'd just lost a chess tournament to me.

"You're not worried about finding a job or anything, are you?" I asked.

"Heavens no," he said.

"I guess the main thing is finding the right job," I said.

He smiled. "The what job? What do you mean, the right job?"

"Well, one that's meaningful."

"Meaningful. What's that? What's a meaningful job?"

"I don't know," I said, thinking I shouldn't have mentioned it after all.

"A job is a job," he said. "I don't know what a meaningful job is. If you find out, you tell me. I'd be interested to know."

"All right," I said.

I let Dad have the rest of my apple pie—he'd been eyeing it. Once he started eating the pie, he didn't want any more beer. When he finished the last crumbs, we went outside in the fresh air and walked around on the gravel. Dad said he wanted to make sure his head was clear, even though he hadn't finished the bottle. The rain was falling softly. During the drive home, Dad listened to the Mariners game while I slept, and when I woke up, we were practically home.

**10**

The next morning I laced up my tennis shoes and went for a run.

I ran down my street, cut through the Mandls' unfenced side yard, loped alongside Marion Creek gurgling by on my left, and hooked up with the Burke-Gilman Trail.

Once upon a time the trail had been miles and miles of railroad tracks; now it was a smoothly paved path with a stripe painted down the middle, one side for wheels, the other side for feet. It worked its way south for thirty-some miles following Lake Washington's shoreline to the University of Washington, then cut west and paralleled the Lake Washington Ship Canal, finally ending up at Seattle's Fremont district. To the north it went umpteen miles all the way to the city of Woodinville and beyond.

I jogged south for about a mile. I was not having fun. My body was in agony—toes, heels, arches, ankles, calves, shins, knees, thighs; my side was splitting; my lungs felt like a ruptured accordion. Even my brain hurt: For some reason a particularly annoying jingle from a TV commercial was playing a continuous loop in my head.

But I chugged along, waiting for that legendary second wind. Which now struck me as bigger bunkum than the infomercial promises offered by the speed-reading courses and My-T-Gym muscle-building machine.

The trail wound through the Briarcrest Beach neighborhood, where I turned off onto the sidewalk, huffing past the stately houses with their putting-green lawns, many of which rolled right down to the waterfront. Coming to the beach club (not yet open), I turned right, recrossed the Burke-Gilman Trail, gasped and staggered up the hill to the next block, and turned left. That put me on Annie's street.

I had always liked her street. Big grandfatherly trees lined both sides. The yards were well kept, and the driveways demanded a basketball hoop if they didn't already have one. The houses were a mixture of traditional and modern, brick and wood, all with great views of Lake Washington, the distant Seattle skyline, and Mount Rainier. Annie's house was halfway down the block on my left. I ran past it to the end of the block, then turned around and ran back the way I had come to the Burke-Gilman Trail. I didn't know why I had run past her house or what I would have done if she'd seen me. My sideache and head-jingle were gone. I jogged another fifty yards, then walked the rest of the way home.

When I got home, I went around to the backyard and started doing push-ups. The unmowed grass came up past my wrists. Do twenty, I commanded myself. At fifteen, my triceps and pecs burned. Five more. They just about killed me. I got up, sweating, swearing, and sore. Then I got down on my back, locked my hands behind my head, and started doing crunches with my knees up in the air, touching my elbows to my knees. My stomach started to cramp at twenty, but I forced myself to do five more. I groaned and lay back flat on the cool grass and looked up at the sky.

I could smell the grass and the fresh wood. Stacked under our deck and around both sides of our house were enough logs to make firewood for the next ten years. The logs were cut in three-foot sections, some almost as big around as a telephone pole. They gave off a rich, sweet smell.

I stood up and found a log that weighed about ten pounds, put my hands on either end of it, and started lifting it over my head, doing overhead presses. I did fifteen of these until my arms ached. Then I did some curls and some upright rows. When I was finished, I heaved the log away and squeezed my biceps to see if they felt bigger. They didn't.

All of this wood had come from a gigantic poplar tree on the property line between our yard and the Daumiers'. There was no fence separating our two yards, and legally the tree had belonged to the Daumiers. The trunk had been huge, going up about ten feet and then branching out into two trees that towered above our roofs.

Every single day of my life, I had looked out my bedroom window at that tree. It was the first thing I saw when I woke up and the last thing I saw when I went to bed, and I could even see it from my bed in the middle of the night, its branches and leaves black against the night sky.

The leaves reflected the seasons, and it gave shade and shelter to our yards. In late September, right around my birthday, its leaves changed color and fell and covered our yards. That was one chore I loved, raking leaves on brisk Saturday afternoons in the fall.

"He's just a big old nuisance," Mr. Daumier had said last winter. "His roots are coming up in my basement, they're cracking the foundation. One of these days, he'll have to go."

That "one of these days" had set me at ease. It meant never, of course.

A crew of three men had shown up on April Fool's Day. The branches of the tree were still bare, the buds hadn't yet sprouted. With the loud continuous roar of the hydraulic engine, the crew started at the top, tying ropes to the bigger branches, cutting it down piece by piece. It took two days. I watched from my bedroom window, in shock. When they were finished, there was just a big hole there. In me, too. Lacy was inconsolable for weeks, grief stricken, but I stayed numb.

Gradually the shock had worn off. Although sometimes still when I looked to where the tree used to be, expecting to see it and not seeing it, I felt sick to my stomach.

The tree was gone. I'd get used to it.

I didn't have any other choice.

August finished out on a series of muggy, humid days, as if we were inside a greenhouse. I ran most days and chose a variety of routes, even though I didn't know what the heck I was in training for. The mornings were foggy, and running through the fog not being able to see anything beyond a few feet was weird and spooky. I preferred the clear evening at twilight, when the sun was gone and the sky yellow and red. Running along the Burke-Gilman Trail, I'd hit patches of fresh, cool air. I'd hit swarms of gnats, too, and I inhaled many. But gnat's another story.

After my run I'd do some push-ups and sit-ups. Then I'd do lifting exercises with logs. Mom finally got around to telling me to mow the lawn, so I did that. I read parts of the Rafer Johnson autobiography. Skeepbo and I hung out at the beach club or at the mall or his house. We practiced for the badminton tournament on Labor Day.

On Saturday evening of Labor Day weekend, the Skeepbos invited me to stay for dinner. Mr. Skeepbo was going to barbecue some fresh Copper River salmon. "Twenty-two bucks a pound," he said. Mr. Skeepbo always broke things down to their unit cost. "Three hundred and seventy-seven bucks a pound" was what the fat farm had cost him, because Aidan had only lost seventeen pounds.

After Skeepbo and I had each eaten twenty-two dollars' worth of salmon, we sat out on the deck and watched the sky and lake change colors as the sun set.

Later we made root beer floats and took them downstairs to the multimedia center and heaved back in our dueling EZ-Man recliners and channel-surfed on the big-screen Mitsubishi. It was a long-standing tradition of ours to set the alarm for twenty minutes. During that time, one person got exclusive control of the channel changer. When the alarm went off, it was the other guy's turn. I kept returning to the self-help channel. I wanted to see the My-T-Gym infomercial again, or the one for the speed-reading program, but I didn't find either one of them.

Skeepbo landed on an old movie called *College Chicks Rock*. It definitely looked 1960s. It was in color, but 1960s color.

There were all these bikini-clad females doing the Mashed Potato on the beach. They were beauties, but by today's standards they would have been considered flabby.

"I wish I'd lived in those days," Skeepbo said. "No such thing as jogging or aerobics. Just a lot of weird dances."

"Dancing is a strange thing," I said, drinking my root beer float.

"It's my theory that dancing was invented for one purpose," Skeepbo said. "Male arousal."

"Works for me," I said.

I left Skeepbo's around ten o'clock. As I walked home, the night air seemed all alive and abuzz. It smelled like the end of summer and pretty girls dancing. I was stirred up. I wanted to drink the air and splash it all over me. I wanted to have a girl, but I doubted I would know what to do with her, and you needed a car and money to go on dates and such, and I wasn't even fifteen yet. I would just have to wait.

**11**

As I approached my house, I saw that it was completely dark—not even the porch light was on. Dad's car was in the driveway, but Mom's wasn't there, which meant either Lacy had borrowed it for work or Mom and Dad had gone out.

Inside, I didn't bother turning on any lights. I moved through the downstairs and into the kitchen and noticed a dark figure standing outside on the deck, leaning against the wooden railing. My dad.

Hesitating, I quietly slid open the glass door and stepped lightly onto the deck.

"Do you mind some company?" I asked.

"Not at all. Come and sit down."

I slid the door closed behind me and sat on one of the deck chairs and put my feet up on the railing. My feet looked big to me.

"Nice night," I said.

"Yeah."

"What are you doing?"

"Remembering my old Volkswagen and a funny hat I used to wear."

A breeze stirred the leaves and touched my face. The stars seemed to brighten for a moment, then dim again. I heard distant voices, laughter, soft piano music.

"Somebody's having a party," I said.

"The Mandls."

"Sounds like a big one."

"Their annual Labor Day weekend bash."

The voices and uproar and piano swelled and subsided. A burst of laughter, dominated by a woman's whooping laugh, floated across the night like bubbles.

"You and Mom didn't go this year?"

"We weren't invited this year."

"Fell out of their social circle, huh?"

Dad chuckled. "More like I punted us out. Back in June, I ran into Beth Mandl at the golf course and said something unforgivably rude to her. Which I will not repeat, so don't bother asking."

"Can I ask why you said it?"

"It was a promise I made to myself. A solemn vow that if Beth Mandl told me one more time the story of how she and Seth were able to *send their Crissi to Princeton because, once upon a time, years and years ago, they bought some stock in a little-bitty company called Microsoft*, I would say something unforgivably rude to her face. And sure enough, she forced me to keep my promise."

He paused for a moment, and we listened to the babble and laughter of the party.

"Ah, life in the suburbs," Dad said.

"What about life in the suburbs?"

"It sneaks up on you and bites you in the ass."

I didn't understand and wasn't sure I wanted to. That was something I'd been noticing lately about Dad. He had been making these statements more often; statements that seemed to come from some dark, sour place in him, with poison barbs on them that I didn't want to touch.

This time, though, he followed it with an explanation: "The suburbs are a place where you wake up one morning and realize you're living a life you vowed in college you would never live." His voice sounded light and without self-pity. He shrugged, and I saw his faint smile as he added, "But what does a college kid know anyway, right?"

I inhaled; the air was sweet and moist and pungent with the smell of fir and pine trees and all that fresh wood that had been the Daumiers' tree.

"We had some good salmon at Skeepbo's," I said.

"Nothing like fresh Copper River salmon on the barbecue."

Just then, in the dark, with Dad beside me, I felt more mature and worldly than usual. I said, "Do you think self-confidence is something you learn, or is it something you have to be born with?"

"Something you learn. As a father I would be doing a disservice to say anything else."

There he went again. Putting that spin on what would otherwise have been a direct answer.

"Do you think some people have a charmed life?" I asked.

"Yes."

I wasn't sure which surprised me more, his answer or his lack of hesitation.

"You think it's possible for somebody to be born under a good sign?" I asked.

"Yes."

"I thought you'd say there's no such thing as a charmed life. That all good things come your way because of prayer and hard work and self-discipline. Those things can be developed and coached. You don't have to be born with them."

"Well said. That would be the party line, all right."

"Which is it, then?" I said.

"Which is what?"

"You say faith and self-confidence can be developed and learned. But you also say a person can be born with a charmed life. Can it be both?"

Dad turned and looked at me. He reached out and put his hand on my head as if to pat me. His hand felt hard and callused from all his golfing. "You're a good kid, you know that? I don't know everything. I don't have all the answers."

"I don't want all the answers," I said. "Just an opinion or two. Yours."

There came a sudden uproarious burst of laughter from the Mandl party, as if they had heard my remark and were reacting to it.

"You need to form your own opinions," Dad said, sitting down next to me. "And make your own decisions."

The laughter stopped and the piano music faded away. The night was still. Dad and I sat in companionable silence.

**12**

The next day was overcast and I went for a run by Annie's house. She was out in the yard mowing her lawn with an electric mower. The orange extension cord ran from the mower through a basement window. She waved when she saw me. I jogged over to her and she let up on the throttle and the mower went quiet.

"I didn't know you were a runner," she said.

"I haven't been doing it for long."

"I thought maybe you had come by to admire my cat door."

"No," I said, smiling.

"All ready for school?" she asked.

"Yeah. How about you?"

"Almost."

I wiped the sweat off my forehead with my T-shirt. "Well, I'll let you get back to your mowing."

"Have a good run," she said.

Back at my house I did some push-ups and sit-ups and log presses. Then I went upstairs and stood before the bathroom mirror flexing and beholding my muscles.

I went into the hall and got the phone and carried it into my room and stepped across my piles of books to my desk. One of these days I would have to clean this room.

I slid open my top desk drawer and found Annie's phone number, which I had written on the wood four years ago, and called the number.

Her mother answered and put Annie on.

I cleared my throat, a nervous habit I had picked up from my dad.

"Hi, this is Gardner Dickinson. Hey, I forgot to ask you if you signed up for the badminton tournament at the beach club tomorrow. I was just curious."

"No, I didn't sign up. Did you?"

"Yeah, Aidan and I are playing doubles. I thought you and Sophie might enter. You guys used to be great at badminton."

"We did?"

"I might have made that up."

"Can you still enter it?"

"Right up to eleven o'clock tomorrow. It starts at noon."

"Well . . . it might be fun. I'll see if Sophie's got anything going tomorrow. Who knows, maybe we really did use to be good at it."

The next day, Skeepbo and I didn't have much trouble advancing through the rounds of the badminton tournament. I was quick and had a good overhead smash, and Skeepbo was light on his feet, well coordinated, and crafty. He had a deadly accurate flick shot and a fake smash that he'd plink over the net at the very last second.

I looked around for Annie. She and Sophie hadn't signed up, but I thought she might come anyway.

Our toughest match was in the semis, where we had our hands full against an aggressive Bee Bixler and a savagely competitive East Indian kid named Chevaly. His arms were about thirteen feet long. You couldn't get anything past him, so our strategy was to hit everything right at him, and it worked. Skeepbo and I won the match 15–12.

For the finals, a surprising number of spectators had gathered. Our opponents had a little sword-fighting routine they did with their rackets, which amused the crowd. But they were no match for Skeepbo and Dickinson; we triumphed. We lifted our rackets to the applauding crowd and accepted our identical trophies featuring a genderless action figure hitting an overhead smash with something about the size and shape of a flat wooden freezy-malt spoon.

I took one last look around for Annie, but she was nowhere.

Skeepbo and I decided to walk over to Briarcrest Village Mall and celebrate with an iced mocha.

We had to wait for a bunch of joggers to go by before we could cross the Burke-Gilman Trail. Two of them were women, both wearing baseball caps with their ponytails sticking out through the hole in the back swinging to and fro. Skeepbo growled.

At the crosswalk at Mall Way, we waited for the ten-thousandth time for the Red Hand to change into a Walking Man. Cars swooshed by. This highway was always heavy with traffic. It was what radio traffic reporters called an "alternate route," as in "Northbound 405 is bumper to bumper, use an alternate route."

When the light finally changed and the traffic stopped, we stepped out into the crosswalk. And it never failed: The Walking Man was immediately replaced by a blinking Red Hand. Some malicious traffic engineer had intentionally programmed it to hurry us along.

We walked past the Dippy Duck Car Wash and Das Pancake Haus, crossing the nearly empty parking lot, and entered the mall.

Steubens coffee shop was designed to resemble a Paris sidewalk café, complete with fake illuminated lampposts. Crowded around a table covered with iced mochas sat the Big Three—Tippy, Starr, and the Aztecan Beauty. Cut-offs, shorts, sundress. Three or four other satellite girls sat on their outskirts, failing to be received into the inner circle.

"It's never too late to improve your mind," Tippy called out to me.

She always said that to me, because over the years she'd often seen me coming to and from the library carrying sacks full of books, and the sacks usually had that slogan printed on them.

"We heard you entered the badminton tournament," Starr said. "How'd you do?"

"We won," I said, trying to sound humble. "We garnered two lovely trophies."

"You what two lovely trophies?" Tippy said.

"Garnered them."

"Garnered them," Tippy mused. "I'll have to add that to my vocab list."

"Where are the trophies?" Starr asked.

"In his backpack," I said.

"Right here in my backpack," Skeepbo said redundantly.

"How did you know we entered the tournament?" I said.

"We have our ways," Starr said. "We are, after all, members of the beach club. At least Tippy and I are."

"Hey, Aidan, how was the cruise?" Tippy asked. "How were the Greek Islands?"

"Still there last time I looked."

"Yeah?" Tippy said, nodding and smiling. She had a hooked nose and one of the most downturned smiles I'd ever seen. "Glad to hear it. How about the cruise ship? Was it like the Love Boat? Tell us about your trip."

Skeepbo and I entered the seating area, and the girls

scooted their chairs to make room for us at their table. We put our stuff down on a couple of chairs, then went up to the counter (nobody was ahead of us in line; such was the beauty of a dead mall) and ordered iced mochas and blueberry muffins, and took them back to the table.

"Not exactly a cheeseburger," Skeepbo said.

All three of the girls laughed at this. I didn't think Skeepbo had meant it to be funny, but the laughter was warm and genuine, and I could tell he was flattered and pleasantly surprised.

I sat down next to the Aztecan Beauty. Skeepbo sat across from me, between Tippy and Starr, who immediately started firing questions at him. We had known Tippy and Starr almost as long as we had known each other. Skeepbo's mother was friends with their mothers.

The Aztecan Beauty, who had only moved here last year in ninth grade, drew her chair closer to me and lowered her voice. She smelled like baby powder.

"Gardner."

I had to think a moment to remember her real name. "Gabriella."

Sitting a foot away from the Aztecan Beauty and having a private conversation with her was not something the average guy did every day.

"We were over at Tyler's today," she purred.

"Gregerson's? Oh, yeah?"

"He's been having these little get-togethers at his house."

"M-hm?"

"I hear you know Annie Harris," she said.

"Yeah?"

"Her and Sophie Beam were there."

"Yeah?" I saw no point in correcting the Aztecan Beauty's grammar.

"Her and Tyler are sort of a thing now."

Again, no grammar correction. And no need for clarification on what a "thing" was.

"Annie?" I said. "Or Sophie?"

She didn't answer this, as if it was obvious, which it was.

I wondered why the Aztecan Beauty was telling me this. Then I wondered if Annie had said something about my calling her. But I couldn't imagine why she'd do that.

I took a sip of iced mocha, puzzled.

"Why are you telling me this?" I asked.

"Oh, just because," she said. "Tippy and Starr told me . . ."

"Told you . . . ?"

"That you and Annie . . ."

"Me and Annie . . . ?" Never mind the grammar.

"I mean . . ." The Aztecan Beauty almost blushed and lowered her voice another notch. "Correct me if I'm wrong, but they told me you and Annie used to have the hots for each other. Back in fifth grade or something? That's the way they said it. I'm just saying what they said. I don't even know her outside of talking to her a few times at Tyler's, which she seemed nice enough. I don't know what went on between she and you but I thought you'd want to know about she and Tyler."

I looked over at Tippy and Starr. They were chattering away with Skeepbo and didn't glance in my direction, but I knew they hadn't missed a word.

"All right, you guys," I said. "What in the heck are you trying to pull, anyway?"

"Nothing, nothing," Starr said innocently.

"Don't go around gossiping about things that aren't true," I said.

"All right, all right," Starr said. "We'll strike it from the records."

"We won't even let it cross our minds," said Tippy.

## 13

The weather on Tuesday, the first day of school, was hot and sunny. Most people wore shorts to school, although I wore my usual jeans.

Annie wasn't in any of my classes. Skeepbo and I only had one class together, Boys' PE. Gregerson was in there, too. (Our school district had gone back and forth on coed versus same-sex PE classes and had finally decided to go with what the overwhelming majority wanted.) During lunch Skeepbo and I ate at a big table where numerous chess games were in progress. After school he was all booked up, mostly because of his trumpet playing: This year he was doing both stage band and marching band, plus taking private lessons. Also, his parents were bribing him into taking a post–fat farm conditioning class at a gym two nights a week. If he stuck with it, his parents would buy him a car for his sixteenth birthday at the end of March. Actually, he was leaning toward a truck. "For us full-figured guys," he said. "And don't worry, my truck will be just as much yours as mine."

He meant it, too. Even though he was a rich, spoiled, pampered brat, he was the best of best friends.

I hadn't even turned fifteen yet. My birthday was still two weeks away. It was my misfortune to have one of the latest birthdays in my class. It came on the day before our school district's cutoff period. If I'd been born a day later, I would have entered kindergarten a year later, and I'd be a normal ninth grader instead of an immature, maldeveloped tenth grader.

During those first three weeks of school, I checked out some after-school clubs—drama and chess. Talk about two extremes! The drama people were boisterous, exuberant, demonstrative; the chess players, hunched over their boards, snickered when they skewered you with their knight or forked your queen.

I had nothing against either group, and I liked that they were from opposite parts of the galaxy. But belonging to a club of any type just didn't light my fire. Nothing did. I tried working out on the Nautilus in the weight room, but it was way overcrowded with off-season junior and senior jocks, so I bagged that.

At home after school, sometimes I'd run into Dad. More often than not he was playing golf, but when he was home, he was usually either reading or out in the garage sorting through his magazines with the boom box playing, or making a halfhearted attempt at housework or a minor fix-it project.

I didn't pay too much attention to his job search, and Dad didn't seem all that interested in talking to me about it. Occasionally at dinner—those few times we did eat dinner together—Mom would ask him if he was making any progress, the same way she asked him about the garage. Dad would shrug and give vague answers.

Mom and Dad would ask me how school was going. I'd shrug and give vague answers.

Mom thought I should turn out for a sport. "It doesn't have to be a varsity sport," she said. "Intramural would be fine. You could even do it at the community center. Look, Gardner, I know you're not going to turn into a hood who hangs around smoking cigarettes. And I know you don't have any problem finding things to do. But you need structure. We all need structure and discipline."

Here—and I'm sure she couldn't help it—she glanced at Dad.

"What you don't seem to understand, Jamie," Dad said to Mom, "is that Gardner wants to find something more than just after-school busywork. He's looking for his passion, his great calling. Right, Gardner?"

"I understand that," Mom said. "But sometimes the best way to find your calling is to be busy—so busy you don't have time to look for your calling. It's a paradox, you see? You can't sit around waiting for it to find you; you can't wait for opportunity to fall into your lap. Which is what you have a tendency to do."

"I believe the word for that is lazy," Dad said.

"No, easygoing," Mom said. "Placid. You don't get all stressed out about things, is all. That's not a bad quality, Cam. But it's not exactly the attitude of a go-getter who's going to set the world on fire."

"What do you want our son to be, a global arsonist? What is this 'set the world on fire' crap?"

"You know what I mean. You don't have to be nasty about it."

" 'Be a go-getter.' 'Set the world on fire.' That's such ad-agency lingo. All those type A go-getter self-important dickheads with their middle-aged ponytails, running off to their power meetings and talking on their goddamned cell phones and acting like their stupid pretentious billboards and thirty-second commercials are some kind of god-damned Shakespearean sonnet."

Dad never swore. Not on the golf course, not in the middle of a traffic jam. True, I wasn't there every minute to monitor him, but I didn't have to be. It was just something I knew about Dad, because I knew Dad.

Finally, I turned fifteen on the third Sunday of September. Mom made a chocolate cake. Skeepbo came over with a present. That was a first. I started right in razzing him about it.

"How come you're getting me a birthday present all of a

sudden?" I said. "Does this mean I have to get you one for your birthday? Is this a new tradition? What did you get me, a locket with your picture in it?"

Dad joined in. "Maybe you two are going to start giving hugs and sending each other little cards that say, 'Just thinking about you.' "

"You two, zip up your mouths," Mom said.

"That's all right," Skeepbo said. "I'm used to mockery."

My folks gave me the running shoes I'd asked for. Good old practical Lacy gave me a wallet. "In the pizza world, they call it a dough holder," she said. Pizza humor. Any joke from my sister was a rare happening.

Skeepbo's present turned out to be a gift certificate for twenty dollars at a sporting goods store. He was thinking I could apply it toward buying a weight-lifting bar with a set of free weights.

"It's a lovely thought," my mom said, "only . . . where in the world would you put it?"

"In my room," I said. "On the floor. I'll make room for it."

That cracked her up. In fact, it cracked everyone up. Except me.

**14**

On Wednesday afternoon of the following week, unpredicted clouds rolled in, making the day go dark and bringing hard steady rain with thunder and lightning. When school got out, there was chaos, people without coats scrambling for rides. I looked forward to walking home, dodging lightning bolts, getting totally drenched.

As I was walking along under the breezeway, passing people waiting for their rides, I came to the far end, and there stood Annie, holding her books against her stomach, staring off into space. She wore a short dress with no jacket.

She'd shown up on Monday of that week with her long summer blond hair chopped off, leaving a dull brown boyish cut barely over her ears. It didn't seem too flattering. It made her neck look longer, her eyes bigger, and her cheeks chubbier.

She seemed preoccupied, but when she saw me she smiled and said, "Happy birthday."

"Thanks. How did you know?"

She shrugged. "I just remembered. Yours comes so late, I guess. Wow, it sure is raining."

I looked out at the rain, then back at Annie. "Uh, nice haircut. Sporty."

"Sporty. Thanks."

"Waiting for a ride?"

"Yeah."

"Well . . ." I said, and started to head out from under the breezeway.

"Hey, Gardner."

I stopped.

"Do you think it's possible not to care what people think about you?" she asked.

"It guess it depends on how many beers you've had."

She smiled limply. "I wish I didn't care what people think."

"You mean your, uh, hair?"

"What about my hair?" She put a hand to it.

"Is that what you wish you didn't care what people think about?"

She laughed. "Thank you, that's the first time I've laughed since I got it cut."

"Why did you get it cut?"

"Did I need to have a reason?"

"Sorry, wrong question to ask. Your day hasn't been so good, huh?"

She shook her head.

"Well, you can vent before your ride gets here if you want."

She hesitated and bit her lower lip, then talked for two minutes. Person X had said that Person Y had said that Person Z had said something mean about Annie, and Annie had signed up to be on the Soph-Phormal Dinner Committee, but now she didn't know whether she wanted to be on the committee if Person Z was going to be on it, that is if Person X was to be believed, and so on. I was nodding.

Finally she stopped and said, "I'm boring you with all this crap."

"That's all right," I said.

She smiled. "You're really walking home in this?"

"Why not? You and I used to walk home and get drenched, remember? We'd stick our heads under downspouts."

"I remember that," she said with a laugh.

A car pulled up, and the passenger half-lowered the window and waved at Annie and Annie waved back, but the car drove off.

"So what did you decide to do?" I asked.

"About what?"

"The Soph-Phormal Dinner. You going to be on the committee or not?"

"I think so."

"I sure would. Not that you asked my opinion."

"I bet you don't even care about the Soph-Phormal Dinner," she said, smiling.

"What a thing to accuse a person of."

"No. You care about dinner, and you maybe care about sophomores. But in the great scheme of things, you don't care about the Soph-Phormal Dinner."

"I suppose not."

"Although," she said, "it is a fund-raiser for more important things. Things like—like getting new shelves for the Video Resource Room and replacement floor tiles for the head cook's office and miniature flags for the model United Nations. The list goes on and on."

"The head cook has her own office? I didn't know that. Actually, I didn't even know we had a head cook."

"So you see, the Soph-Phormal Dinner is important. Somebody has to organize it."

"Then it should be you," I said. "You should spearhead that committee. It would be a feather in your cap. A gigantic feather. It will prepare you for being a future fund-raiser of America."

"Hey, don't laugh. My mother makes a good living at it."

"At what? Fund-raising? Seriously?"

"Seriously. That's her job. She gets hired by charities and nonprofit groups to scrounge up money for them."

More cars cruised by, but none seemed to be Annie's ride. I almost turned to go but lingered.

"Hey, Gardner," she said. "I'm sorry I didn't make it to the badminton tournament. I actually was going to go, whether Sophie wanted to enter the tournament or not. But then the next day, something else came up."

"That's all right."

"The truth is, three weeks ago, when you called, I was so infatuated with Tyler Gregerson, I would have bumped the Pope for him."

"Not the Pope."

"Yes."

"Are you still infatuated with him? You can tell me it's none of my business."

"Still infatuated with who?"

"Tyler."

"Tyler who."

"Ah, now I get it. You used him for his ski boat, but when the weather turned sour, so did your affections."

"That's right. We're ancient history."

More cars drove by, more people got picked up, and the number of people standing around dwindled.

"I don't think your ride's showing up," I said. "In fact, I'm starting to think you don't have a ride. I bet you were just standing here waiting for people to come up and tell you they like your haircut."

"And let me spout off about the Soph-Phormal Dinner."

"You wanna walk home and stick our heads under a few downspouts? At least it'll only take you about three seconds to dry your hair."

"I do have a ride. How about another time?"

"Okay. Who's your ride?"

"A guy I met last Friday."

"Pre or post haircut?"

"Pre."

"He's in for a shock."

"Thanks. I think I know that already."

"Where'd you meet him?"

"My mother took me to a silent-auction fund-raiser for the Seattle Symphony. I met him there. He goes to Ambalm Prep."

"Did you buy anything at the auction?"

"This haircut."

"Oh."

"Ever heard of Ambalm Prep?" she asked.

"Sure."

"What is it? I've never heard of it."

"It's a private school for spoiled rich people, tucked away in the Madrona neighborhood, only about two miles from the house where Kurt Cobain shot himself."

"That's an interesting bit of trivia," she said.

"Do you want me to go so he doesn't drive up and see you talking to a real stud?"

"That's okay. We'll let him be jealous. You're the one he'll kill. Me he'll just smack around, teach me not to talk to other studs."

I was curious to see this guy from Ambalm Prep.

"So what do you do after school?" Annie said. "Where's Aidan?"

"Marching band practice. I don't do much."

"Have you tried any after-school clubs?"

"Chess, drama, and weight lifting. I'm thinking next I'll try the book club. I heard they're meeting tomorrow. Not only is it a book club, it's a competitive team. They have interleague matches against other schools."

"No way."

"I'm not kidding."

"How could the book club have matches against other teams?"

"All the schools are given the same list of books to read in advance. When the interleague competitions start, each team selects four representatives. A panel of judges asks them questions about some of the books that are on that advance list, and the team reps, they don't know which books the judges will ask them about."

"You're not making that up?"

I was about to say something, when a black car drove up to the curb and stopped about ten feet to our left. This had to be the one. The car was a Lexus. The driver had hip hexagonal glasses and a Bill Gates haircut.

"That's him," she said. "He's going to hate my hair."

The guy was scanning the walkway for the long-haired version of the girl he'd hit on Friday night. Then at last, his eyes landed on the new Annie. Recognition. Surprise. Then a big grin. He eased the car forward directly in front of us. He had to lean against his steering wheel to see the stud Annie was talking to. Now he saw that I was no stud. He wouldn't have to kill me and beat Annie.

"Well, he didn't flee when he saw your hair," I said.

She gave me a quick smile, then stepped forward to the car and opened the door, allowing Kenny G music to escape as she got in. She waved. I waved back. They drove away.

It was too good. A black Lexus and Kenny G. I smiled and shook my head and started home in the rain.

**15**

Dad's car was in the driveway. The garage door was open and the ceiling light was on, but he wasn't in there. The side door leading into the kitchen was unlocked.

I took off my wet clothes and left everything but my boxer shorts on the pantry floor by the washer and dryer, grabbed a towel from a pile of unfolded laundry, and started drying myself off. I could hear the wind outside lashing the rain against the house.

Back in the kitchen, I called out to my dad again, but all was still and dark.

On into the living room. I stood at the foot of the stairs, looking up. It wasn't until I had turned seven years old that I'd been able to go upstairs by myself without being afraid. It must have been some developmental thing in my brain. Before that, even if Mom or Lacy or Dad was home, I'd have to make one of them stand at the foot of the stairs and wait for me.

And although I wouldn't have admitted it to another living person, not even Skeepbo, even now, at fifteen years old, there were certain moments on dark gloomy afternoons . . .

"Dad?"

No answer.

Telling myself not to be a wimp, I climbed the stairs, passing family photos that lined one wall of the stairway. I noticed how dusty they'd gotten these past few months.

At the top, I flipped on the hall light. The door to my parents' bedroom was partly open. I glanced in and got a chill.

Dad was in there.

He was sitting at the desk in the dark room. His body was facing the dead computer screen, but his head was turned to the window, his eyes staring at the rain beating against the glass.

I stepped to the doorway.

"I didn't think you were home," I said.

He didn't move. The rain streaming down the window made shadows that were projected on the walls, making the walls look alive with squiggling snakes.

"Dad?"

"I was just sitting here."

I stood in my boxers, holding the towel against my chest. Water drops ran down my back.

"Just doing some thinking," he said. "Peeling away the layers of the onion, you might say."

"I'll leave you to it."

"No, no, come in, sit down. It's been a while since we've had a talk."

"I'll put some clothes on. I got drenched walking home."

In my room I put on a T-shirt and pair of sweats. I glanced out my window into the backyard, where the tree used to be.

Back in my parents' room, I sat on the edge of the bed.

"Dark in here," I said, trying to sound lighthearted. I almost told him about the Lexus and the Kenny G music. Dad would have been suitably nauseated by it. But it was probably one of those things you had to be there to appreciate.

We sat watching the rain.

"Anything new with you?" I said.

"Hm?"

"Had any nibbles?"

"Nibbles?"

"The job search."

"Oh."

Dad kept watching the rain. He seemed to be somewhere else. We just sat there, but I didn't feel he wanted me to leave.

Finally, Dad said, "I've been wondering how it is I happen to be sitting here on a Wednesday afternoon in a darkened bedroom, looking out the window. That shouldn't be too hard to figure out, should it?"

I didn't say anything. After a few seconds' pause, Dad went on.

"It isn't that I've taken a lot of wrong turns or made bad moves. At least, I don't think so. But here I am. How in the world did I get here?"

His tone sounded light and baffled, a touch amused, as if he were telling about the 8 that he'd shot on some par-4 hole.

"I'm forty-nine," he said. "Unbelievable."

"That's not that old," I said.

"What have I done with all these years?"

"Come on," I said.

Dad smiled, shook his head. "Forty-nine."

"That's not that old at all. You're only as old as you feel."

"Gardner, I'm not looking to be cheered up, so you can spare me the inane platitudes." There was an edge to his voice this time. "I'm trying to be honest for a change."

For a change?

"I don't have much to show for my life. Not many great moments. Same job for seventeen years, I must have been walking around in a fog, sleepwalking. How'd I let all that time— Jeez, look at the rain come down now."

It was slamming into the window in a frenzy. Gusts of wind rocked the house.

"Ho-ly cripe," Dad said.

The room was even darker than it had been five minutes ago. His face looked wan and haggard. He hadn't shaved for several days.

"When you're a kid," he said, "you get all this encouragement and praise. 'Good job! Way to go! You're special!' You start out thinking you can do anything, be great. God is watching over you, steering and guiding your life. You say to yourself, 'I matter. I'm special. The world will notice me because I stand out.' "

Dad shifted in his chair. Outside, the downspouts were gushing.

"Gradually, you start to realize you don't stand out."

Another pause. Dad was smiling vacantly, looking at nothing.

"When I was your age, I was psyched. Just point me in a direction. Any direction. Only somehow I never got pointed. I just kept twisting in the wind. What happened? It strikes me I've spent most of my life waiting. You know that expression, 'waiting for your ship to come in'?" He half-turned and faced me.

I nodded.

"I'll tell you, Gardner—and this is no reflection on you or your mom or Lacy—but I'll be honest with you. I don't really like my life very much. And I don't know what to do."

He stopped. His words stayed in the air. I felt the blood drain from my face.

Dad and I sat there a few more minutes. Finally he slapped his thighs, stood up, and walked out.

I went to my room and stretched out on my bed and lay looking up at the ceiling for a long time.

**16**

The next day after school, I went and sat in on the book club meeting. I had figured there'd be a turnout of maybe five brainy girls sitting primly at desks reading *Jane Eyre*. I was surprised to find a room filled with average, boisterous people of both sexes.

But I was really only half there. I'd been thinking all day about my dad. He had let me see a side of him that I had never seen before. He had made me his confidant and opened himself up to me. Did he really think his life was a failure?

When the meeting finally let out, I figured I'd walk home and take a run on the Burke-Gilman.

Annie was coming out of a classroom. The Soph-Phormal Dinner Committee meeting had just ended. We walked down the hall together.

"How are you getting home?" she asked. "Walking?"

I nodded.

"You mind if I walk with you?" she asked. "It's such a nice fall afternoon. No downspouts today, though."

When we got outside, I noticed for the first time that it was a beautiful day.

We started down the street. She seemed to speed up. She took such long strides, she started to pull ahead of me. I didn't try to keep up with her. If she was in that big a hurry, she could go by herself.

"Hey, is this a race or something?" I said.

Annie downshifted. "Sorry, I guess I had too much pent-up energy from that meeting."

We jaywalked across the street and turned down a side street. The afternoon air was fresh after yesterday's storm. Damp brown leaves lay curling in piles on the sidewalk. One of the houses had smoke rising from its chimney. Holes in the cloud covering revealed blue sky.

"You've got a good long stride," I said. "You should turn out for the track team. I'm serious."

"I did. Every year since sixth grade. Hurdles and distance. Cross-country, too."

"Cross-country season is now," I said. "How come you didn't turn out at this school?"

She didn't answer. After a long pause she said, "I used to love running. Especially through the woods."

"Used to?" I wondered what the story was, but I didn't press it.

We passed an old man raking leaves in his yard. He tipped his hat to us, as though he were an extra in a movie. Farther down the street, a kid was kicking a soccer ball against his garage door, making a pattern of circles on the flat wood surface. Next block, we spotted a pair of sneakers tied together by the shoelaces, dangling from the overhead power lines.

We kicked the leaves ahead of us. That was the only sound, our feet swishing through the damp leaves.

"How did your date go?" I asked.

"Which one?"

"How many dates did you have last night?"

"Oh, it was all right."

"Did he like your hair?"

"Raved about it."

"What a phony."

She punched my arm lightly.

"Look." Annie stopped and gazed up at the sky. A giant V-formation of geese was flying overhead. We could hear their honking and their wings whistling. "Go, geese," she said quietly.

"Long may you fly," I said, and it made me shudder because it sounded so corny. It made me sad, too, and I didn't know why.

We walked the rest of the way without saying much. I think we were both glad to stay quiet and enjoy the walk.

That afternoon I was a little nervous, not sure of how I'd find my dad. I found him in a totally messy kitchen, surrounded by bags of groceries on the kitchen floor, every cupboard door open.

"Hey, something smells good," I said, trying to sound upbeat. "You're cooking dinner. Wow. It looks like . . . uh, some kind of rice thing. Pretty impressive, Dad. What's it called?"

"Some kind of rice thing."

"Mom'll be excited."

" 'Excited' may be stretching it."

Boxes of frozen TV dinners were stacked up on the counter, waiting to be jammed into the freezer.

"Need some help putting the groceries away?" I asked.

"How about you fold the sacks as I empty them? I hate folding sacks."

I started on the ones he'd already unpacked. I glanced at him once or twice. He caught me checking him out.

"Nice change in the weather today," he said.

"That's for sure."

"I have to take the laundry out of the dryer."

"I'll help you."

I followed him into the pantry. Dirty clothes, including the wet ones I'd shed yesterday, were distributed in several small piles. They reminded me of the piles of books in my room.

I felt sad seeing my dad stooping to household drudgery when he should have been slaying dragons and amassing a fortune. Or at least using his intelligence. But why hadn't I ever felt that way about my mom? And why did I feel sad for her that she had to work outside the house? Maybe it was just a matter of what I had gotten used to over the years.

Dad pulled the clothes from the dryer and dropped them on the floor. Then he took the load of clothes from the washer and transferred them into the dryer and turned it on. He loaded a new pile of dirty clothes into the washer, added a scoop of detergent, and spun the dial of the washing machine. Then he crouched on the floor and started folding the clean clothes. I hopped up and sat on top of the dryer.

"So, what've you been doing today?" he asked. "Anything exciting?" His face was stubbled with whiskers.

"No, not really," I said. I thought of Annie and I thought of the geese, but I didn't feel like bringing that up. "I went to the book club meeting."

"Yeah? How was that?"

"It was okay. But I don't think it's really for me."

"Oh. That's too bad."

The washing machine shifted into its noisy wash cycle and started chugging and wobbling.

"Hey, Gardner, I was a little off my stride yesterday. I hope it didn't spook you."

"No," I said.

"I want you to know you can always talk to me—about anything. I might not have all the answers, but I can listen. That's my number-one job. I don't want to lose our—our friendship. You're at that age, you know, where kids start to distance themselves from their parents. I want us to be comfortable enough to confide in each other. I don't want us to become strangers."

"All right," I said. "Thanks."

I watched as he continued folding clothes.

"There's something I've been wondering," I said. "I have a pretty dumb question."

"My favorite kind. Shoot."

"Well, I don't know what you actually . . . did."

"Did?"

"I mean, your job. What you did when you, you know—worked. I know you worked for King County. You had an office of your own, right?"

"Yes. It was pretty small, though. More like a cubicle."

"King County, that's part of the local government, right? Federal, state, and local."

"Right. Which has about a million departments. My department, the purpose of my department, basically, was to receive, process, and maintain various requisition forms from other departments, for various pieces of equipment."

"I see," I said, nodding.

"We never saw the actual equipment, only the forms. One day our entire department was eliminated with one stroke of the county exec's pen."

"What did you actually do? How did you spend your day?"

"Oh, I'd get various types of requests and sort them." Dad looked around. "Kind of like I'm sorting this laundry."

"Into piles?"

"Yes. I had to prioritize them."

"What did you—"

"And sometimes a different department would send a request asking about the status of a particular form. That was called an SRF—Status Request Form. SRFs were my special babies. I'm sorry, I interrupted you. What were you going to ask?"

"What did you usually eat for lunch?"

"Oh, sandwiches. Sometimes a group of us would go out."

"Did Mom make your lunch?"

"Sometimes. Not always."

"But the job, it was—uh, you'd have to say it was a fairly important job, right?"

"No." Dad laughed. "I wouldn't say that."

"Do you miss it?"

"About as much as I miss dry heaves."

"How did you get it? I mean, of all the things you could have done, why did you go to work for the county?"

Dad shook his head. "I'm not sure. I needed to settle down. It was a good, stable job, good benefits."

"A job is a job, right?" I said. "But still, what would you do? If you could do anything?"

"If I could do anything? I assume you mean anything within reason, since my first choice would be to play golf for a living, which will have to be in my next life. So besides golf, let's see . . . I've always had this fantasy of being a long-distance trucker. Be out on the open road, pedal to the metal. Talk on the old CB. Pull over at truck stops and drink coffee at the counter and flirt with waitresses."

Dad tossed two bras into the laundry basket.

"But you have a college education," I said. "You know German and Latin. You've studied all these different subjects. It seems like you ought to be working in some high-powered office or something."

"I wouldn't mind being a lumberjack," Dad said, musing. "Felling trees. Swinging an ax. You want to build some muscles, you should try that sometime, chopping wood."

"Really?"

"You bet. I think we've got an ax somewhere in the garage. Or you know what else has always sounded good to me? Having a paper route. I—"

"Oh, yeah."

"No, I mean it. Being outdoors every day, physically active, people actually relying on you for something. Getting to know the customers and the names of their dogs. Making a difference in people's lives. Start your route with a clear, definite purpose; end it with a sense of accomplishment."

He was serious. I didn't know whether to pity him or laugh at him. A grown man actually getting excited at the idea of becoming a paper boy . . .

Dad was losing it. Going off the deep end.

I hopped off the dryer.

"Maybe you should get away for a while," I said. "Go

somewhere for a couple of days and do some good hiking. Before the weather turns. I'd go with you if you wanted, or you could just go by yourself."

"That's not a bad idea," Dad said. "We'll have to do that one of these days. We ought to be able to talk without having to shout over a darn washing machine, shouldn't we."

## 17

After school the next day I looked for the ax in the garage and found it leaning against one wall behind the workbench. I ran my thumb along the blade. I couldn't tell if it was sharp or not. It didn't seem to be.

I took it out to the backyard and picked up a log of the Daumiers' tree and spat in my hands and rubbed them together because that's what I'd seen woodchoppers do, and I started chopping. At first my aim was bad and I couldn't hit the same place twice. Wood chips flew up, and an occasional one hit my face and came close to my eyes, and I thought I'd better wear my sunglasses or some safety goggles but I just squinted my eyes and kept chopping. The sound of the blade on the wood rang out, and the birds and squirrels seemed to have stopped whatever they were doing to listen. Maybe it was an old familiar sound to them that they had never actually heard but knew just the same. I smiled at that thought.

I had a good sweat going. My aim started to get better, and I got so that I could angle the blade left, then right. The V-shaped gash in the log got deeper. I switched hands and tried bringing the ax up over my left shoulder and my aim got bad again but I kept at it. A blister opened up in my left palm, but I kept chopping.

When the gash was more than halfway through the log, I turned the log over and started chopping the other side, forming a new gash, working my way to the center of the log. Eventually the two gashes had just about met, there was only a little bit of wood between them. And then one more swing, and I was through it, the log broke in two.

Now I picked up one of the halves and stood it up on its flat end, with the pointy, freshly chopped end up in the air, and I started chopping down on it lengthwise so as to split it into quarter-sized sections that would fit in the fireplace. This was frustrating because the blade kept wanting to get stuck in the wood and I had to wiggle it up and down to pry it out. So instead, when the blade got stuck, I tried lifting the whole log up over my head and slamming it down on the ground, and this worked better, and eventually I was able to split the log, and I had me some firewood.

I kept chopping all afternoon. It was hard work and satisfying and not a bit boring. Sometimes I got into such a good groove that I went into a kind of trance. I took my shirt off. I was sweating all over. I found some work gloves in the basement and put them on, but my palms were raw and stung with fresh blisters.

The first few days of chopping wood, my whole body was stiff and sore, not just my arms and hands but muscles in my shoulders, my upper and lower back, my butt muscles, and all through my legs. The blisters in my palms hardened into calluses. I took the ax and had the blade sharpened, and I bought some safety glasses so I could watch the chips hit me in the face. While I chopped, my mind would go off into wild fantasies. So I worked on trying to discipline and control my thoughts while I chopped wood. I made up mental puzzles or chess problems or stories or poems, or I debated both sides of an issue, or I tried to remember all the presidents or state capitals—all kinds of things.

Mr. Daumier came out one afternoon and watched me from his yard, smoking his pipe.

"I don't suppose you want to borrow my chain saw," he said.

No, I told him. He said I could help myself to the logs in his yard, too, and I thanked him. Then he said with winter coming, he knew plenty of retired folks who usually bought firewood from the grocery store and would buy it from me so long as I charged less and included some kindling with each bundle like the supermarket did. And the following week I delivered my first load of firewood by wheelbarrow to an old couple three blocks away. I stacked it up along the side of their house, and they paid me in cash.

The fall days passed, and I went running after school or

chopped wood, and I made a little money selling firewood. With that and the gift certificate Skeepbo had given me for my birthday, I bought a curl bar and a stack of five-pound weights to go on each end of it. I had to clean my room to make a place for it, so I gathered up all the library books and hauled them back to the library and settled up my fines. I started lifting weights three times a week.

Skeepbo and I still saw each other, but he was pretty busy. I talked to Annie every now and then. One day in mid-October we were talking about nothing in particular, and we got to talking about running, and I mentioned I was running pretty regularly, and I said we ought to go for a run sometime. She surprised me by saying, "All right, how about this afternoon, after my Soph-Phormal Committee meeting?"

When I mentioned it to Skeepbo later that day, he whistled and said, "Your first date."

"Not a date," I said.

"Tell that to Tippy and Starr."

I had agreed to meet Annie at her house at four-thirty, so I headed for home in the drizzling rain, but first I decided to stop at the library. Ms. Patterson wasn't there, it was her day off. Ms. Pasco was busy helping students with homework assignments.

I sat down in a reading chair by the magazines. I had an hour or so until I had to go home and put on my running stuff and meet Annie.

I picked up a magazine with a sexy girl on the cover but

put it down quickly when I saw that Ms. Pasco was eyeing me from across the room.

Next to the magazine I noticed a book that someone must have pulled from the stacks but not checked out. *Little House on the Prairie*. A girl book. Somewhere in my memory I knew my sister had read the whole series before she had turned eight.

I picked up the book and inspected the cover. I glanced over at Ms. Pasco. She tipped her head to one side and waved to me. I waved back.

I opened the book to chapter one.

*Going West*

*A long time ago, when all the grandfathers and grandmothers of today were little boys and little girls or very small babies, or perhaps not even born, Pa and Ma and Mary and Laura and Baby Carrie left their little house in the Big Woods of Wisconsin. They drove away and left it lonely and empty in the clearing among the big trees, and they never saw that little house again.*

I stopped and looked up.

I closed the book and put it down on the table.

I sat there and thought of my own family. Pa, Ma, Lacy, me. I thought of our two-story, three-bedroom house. My neighborhood was modest, yet it was bordered by Briarcrest Beach, Briarcrest Hills, and Briarcrest Village. Surrounded by affluence.

Life in the suburbs . . .

Our house was the only one I'd ever lived in. Pretty much as long as I could remember, my parents had talked about "someday" moving to a bigger house because we had "outgrown" this one.

I had never quite understood what it meant for a family to outgrow a house.

I looked at the book on the table, picked it back up, and read the first paragraph again. Why was this book considered such a classic? It seemed to violate a lot of the rules of good writing that we had been learning in English, such as using adjectives sparingly and nonrepetitively. Little boys . . . little girls . . . small babies . . . little house . . . Big Woods . . . lonely empty . . . big trees . . . little house.

Yet I liked the words and I liked the style, and when I read the paragraph a third time, the words and rhythm and voice seemed to work their way into me, and I settled back in the chair, and without thinking anymore about whether it was a girl book or a good book, I read the first six chapters. I saw the prairie and felt the rough wool of Pa's shirt, tasted the pancakes and molasses, heard the tapping of forks on tin plates and the whickerings and nickerings of horses.

When I came to the end of chapter six, I got up, stretched, and looked at the clock. It was almost four-thirty. I'd been reading for an hour.

I took the book over to the checkout counter. Ching's replacement, a grandmotherly lady with an English accent, looked at the book, then at me, then back at the book. I almost lied and told her I was getting it for my little sister, but I said nothing.

I walked home and put on my running shoes and shorts and jogged over to Annie's house, just as she was getting dropped off by a fellow committee member's mother.

She led me inside her house to wait for her while she changed. No one was home.

"I'll just be a jiffy," she said.

"Be as many jiffies as you want," I said.

While I waited for her, I looked around the house. It was like a museum. White carpet, white walls, high ceilings—paintings, sculptures, vases everywhere. Annie's mother was quite a collector.

I noticed a particularly intriguing painting. It was a huge canvas, all white, except for several brown streaks. It looked as though it had been left on the floor and a dog had come along and scraped its bottom back and forth across it.

Annie returned wearing running attire and that familiar fresh soap scent. We ran through Briarcrest Beach. She ran effortlessly, as if she'd been entering marathons all her life. She told me something she hadn't told me before: Her father, Ron Harris, had been the state high school cross-country champion. He was still an avid runner, and Annie used to go running with him a lot.

"From my mom I inherited a talent for raising funds, serving on committees, and picking up rich guys at benefit auctions," Annie said. "And from my dad I inherited running."

"And that's why you didn't turn out for cross-country," I said. "You're mad at him and getting back at him."

There was no need for her to say anything to that. After a while she said, "I'm glad I'm running today. I've missed it."

"Me too," I said. "Glad you're running."

We ran down the center of the street in the twilight, past houses that were decorated for Halloween with bats, spiderwebs, witches, and pumpkins. Election signs were clustered on street corners and in some of the front yards. Leaves scuttled across the street. We could see our breath, and we could smell woodsmoke and hear dogs barking in distant yards and hear the faint whiny growl of chain saws.

That was the only time Annie went running with me after school. She had too much else going on and too many people wanting her, too many guys waiting in line to go out with her. Occasionally, though, she joined me on a Saturday or Sunday morning, and we'd run to our high school and follow the cross-country course through the woods. But it started to get too muddy for that.

November came and the days got shorter and it rained just about every day. I still didn't have a clue what I was in training for, but every day I either chopped wood, lifted the weights in my room, or ran. I actually seemed to be getting some muscles.

What was it that had finally turned me around? What was

driving me? I didn't want to think about it too much, because I didn't want to jinx it; I didn't want to make it go away.

All the working out I was doing, letting my thoughts roam free, must have been making my mind stronger and my concentration better. I had finished *Little House on the Prairie*, so I went back to the library and checked out that Rafer Johnson autobiography again and this time read it straight through. What a feeling of accomplishment, to finish another book! Better than winning a long, grueling chess match—better than winning a race.

Then, during a ten-minute free-write in English, I wrote a poem. I wasn't about to argue that it was any literary masterpiece, but what was incredible about it was that it had come from a different place in me, the same place I went in my mind while I was chopping wood or running. I stood up and read the poem to the rest of the class during Sharing.

> *Rain dripping off chrome handlebars*
> *of a red bike with training wheels*
> *turned to watch the boy*
> *walking away.*

"Interesting," Mrs. Lambright said. She cast her eyes around the classroom. "Anyone care to offer an interpretation?"

"I think it's about a bike getting rained on."

"A bike with training wheels."

"A neglected bike."

"Yeah. I can see the drops all lined up on the handlebars. And the handlebars are turned. Like they're watching that boy walk away. I seen bikes do that."

"The boy, he's walking away from his old bike."

"Leaving it behind."

"Maybe he's growing up."

"He's outgrown the bike, yeah. It has training wheels, remember?"

"The bike is sad, and that makes me sad."

"Sad for the bike?"

"Yeah, but for the boy, too. The boy's childhood is ending. He's like, passed through that phase of his life and is moving on to another."

"Whoa, heavy."

"I feel sad when I leave something behind, when I outgrow something."

"Hey, maybe one of his parents is watching the boy walk away from home and childhood or something. Whoa. Did I say that?"

"Maybe it was the parent who wrote the poem, and we're seeing it through the parent's eyes."

"Have you ever been sad to outgrow something?"

"I had a doll."

"My mitt."

"My bong."

"My blankie, man. I had this old blankie when I was little."

"My comic books."

Mrs. Lambright was glowing. "Tomorrow, why don't we come in first thing and write a few paragraphs on childhood and what it means to grow up, to outgrow it."

The class groaned and gave me a collective dirty look.

## 18

I guess Lacy had been right with her prediction about our family. We were all doing our own thing. I don't know how Dad was spending his time, but when he was home, he seemed distant. Mom was working long hours, coming home, crashing. Occasionally she'd get together with her girls' club or co-workers.

Lacy was hardly ever home. Not only was she wrapped up in school and her job, but she had started seeing someone on the sly. The guy she was seeing was her twenty-eight-year-old boss at Pizza Corner, Fritz.

I couldn't believe Lacy could be so stupid as to get involved with an older man who was also her boss.

I wasn't sure whether Mom even knew it was going on.

One weeknight in mid-November, having eaten my microwaved TV dinner, I was sitting at the kitchen table doing some homework when Mom came home around eight o'clock from another one of her thirteen-hour workdays.

As usual she greeted me and asked me about my day, went through the mail, played back the saved messages on the answering machine, downed a couple of aspirins with a glass of water, opened the refrigerator, and poked her head inside. "I'm starving. Anything for dinner?"

I didn't know how to answer this. My own TV dinner had been satisfying enough, but it seemed like an insult for me to suggest to my mother that she microwave a TV dinner.

"Hm, not a whole lot in here," she said, still inspecting the refrigerator. She went to the cupboard and took down a can of soup and stuck it under the electric can opener.

Dad strolled in. His hands were in his pockets.

"I didn't have time to fix anything," he said.

"I had a huge lunch," Mom said. "God, I don't know how some of those clients can eat those big huge lunches all the time." She poured the soup into a pot and put it on the stove.

"Why don't you just microwave it?" Dad said.

"Because soup is one thing I like heated up the old-fashioned way."

"How was traffic?"

"Not bad this time of night."

"That's right—I keep forgetting you miss the evening rush hour because you work so late."

"I'd rather take the bus, but I have to do so much driving around and meeting with clients during the day."

"There we go with the clients again."

"What?"

"That's twice in one minute you've mentioned your clients."

"O-kay." Mom's eyes shifted left and right. "I won't mention the clients again."

"I'm sorry you have to spend all your time driving," Dad said.

"I don't mind it so much. I've been getting those books on tape from the library, you know? They're great. I just finished a book about Napoleon. I've been listening to books I normally wouldn't read. *Moby-Dick, Bleak House, Middlemarch.* Those wouldn't be my first choices to read at home, and I know I wouldn't read them on the bus."

"You've already read *Middlemarch*. You read it in college."

"That's nice of you to remember. It's been a while since college, though. I enjoyed rereading it."

"You mean listening to it. Not reading it." Dad paced the kitchen as if he were caged in. His tennis shoes squeaked. He wasn't wearing any socks. "So commuting is tolerable now, eh? Well, that's good, that's peachy. You know, there's no difference in taste between microwaving your soup and heating it on the stove."

"I think there is. It's probably just psychological."

"You just like doing things the slow, old-fashioned way, that it? You're an all-natural kind of gal."

"Yep, that's me."

I wanted to tell Dad to back off. I also wanted to get up

and leave. But Dad looked so strange to me, part of me was eerily fascinated.

"Poor Jamie," he said. "Has to commute all that way. But she makes the most of it. She listens to books!"

Mom ignored him.

"Poor Jamie. Doesn't have time to read real books the old-fashioned way. Has to have power lunches with her fat-cat clients, with an expense account supplied by her hotshot boss."

Finally, Mom faced him. "Why are you trying so hard to pick a fight with me?"

Dad rolled his eyes in my direction. His face had an unnatural, twisted grin. "You see what she's doing? Heating up her soup on the stove. She's doing that for sympathy. She has to be the martyr. Talking about Napoleon and *Middlemarch* on tape . . . If she didn't have to drive all that way to and from work . . . She's being forced to listen to books on . . . She could be here at home, like she used to be, spending her afternoons having cups of tea and reading real books the old-fashioned way."

"And cooking dinner," Mom said. "And cleaning. And buying groceries. And doing the laundry. And running errands. And being here to at least say hello to my kids during the daylight hours."

"With a big plate of homemade cookies and a glass of milk and a warm smile."

"Hey, at least I made an effort. That's more than you do. You're sure never around here for them."

"How do you know when I'm around? Where's the surveillance camera?"

"I don't need one to know you don't do diddly around here. I haven't complained about your lousy dinners yet, have I? I haven't reminded you that we're well into the month of November and you haven't even come close to—" She stopped.

"Getting a job?" Dad said.

"You haven't even interviewed, Cam."

"No. No, I haven't."

"I don't know what your plan is. I haven't pushed you. I've let you have your space. You have things to work out, that's fine, work them out. Go get some help if you need it. Go see someone. But don't attack me. I'm on your side."

"No, you're right," Dad said, his voice turning vague. "You don't deserve that kind of treatment. And you certainly don't deserve having a worthless bum for a husband."

He walked out of the kitchen. Mom's soup was boiling over.

19

That Saturday Annie and I went for a three-mile run on the Burke-Gilman Trail. It was a gray drizzly morning, and there wasn't much traffic on the trail except for an occasional cyclist passing us on our left. We both wore sweatshirts and sweatpants, and she wore gloves but I didn't. As we ran side by side, I found myself telling her about my dad. She was the only person I could talk to besides Skeepbo, and I couldn't talk to Skeepbo about this.

I had to admit I was worried about my dad. I told her about that weird time in his room during the storm. Then I told her about the incident with Mom.

"I don't understand what's going on with him," I said. We slowed down to a leisurely pace. "One minute he's on the attack, and the next he's like a wounded puppy."

"Why don't you talk to him?" Annie said.

"Me?"

"Yeah, maybe you could sit down and talk to him. Maybe he wants to confide in you."

"I don't want that again," I said. "I don't want to hear him tell me what a bum and a failure he is. Hell, he's my father. I don't want my own father spilling his guts out to me. No way. That would be like—like the President of the United States coming on nationwide TV and getting all weepy and blubbery."

"No, it wouldn't. Gardner, it's not the same thing at all."

"Sure it is. A world leader is supposed to maintain a strong public image, and so is a father. I'm the one who should be spilling my guts out to him," I said. "I'm the kid. He should be giving me support. That's his damn job. Besides, if anybody should talk to him, it should be my sister. If he's going to spill his guts, he needs a woman to clean them up."

"No, it should be you. He needs you. He won't spill his guts."

"Besides, he goes out with his buddies from high school and college. He probably does all the talking and confiding he wants to them."

"You and Aidan are best friends, and you don't exactly have heart-to-heart talks, do you?"

"No. But I still say it's not my place. The father is the hero figure, and the son should look up to him. I'm a kid. I shouldn't have to be burdened by my parents' problems. I should be allowed to be blissfully ignorant, at least until I'm old enough to vote."

"Your dad's just human," she said. "You know that."

"That must be true for your dad, too, then," I said.

Annie didn't say anything. We ran along the trail, past the row of trees on our right and houses on our left, with Lake Washington beyond.

"What was it like having your dad move out?" I asked. "Seeing him pack up and go?"

"I think I went into shock first," she said. "The same as how you described yourself when they chopped your tree down. I think your brain must have a way of protecting you by going numb. But then the numbness starts to wear off. That's when I started to hate him. I know I don't really hate him. Or it's a combination of love and hate. I'd rather be numb again. I'd rather be totally indifferent about him. Sometimes I just want to crawl into a corner and suck my thumb."

"I can't even imagine it," I said. "Having your parents split up. That tree isn't any comparison. Except sometimes I still look out the window and expect to see it there, and when I don't see it, it's like, wow, I get this jolt. But I guess time passes and you get used to it, right? I guess we can adapt to anything."

"I guess," she said. "At least part of you does. But part of you never does. I mean, sure, we don't have much choice. Things change, and we either get used to it or we—or we shut down. But that other part of you still can't quite believe it's happened and won't accept it. I think your mind always has two parts, you know? Like with dying. There's the part that knows you're going to die someday, we're all going to die. But the other part can't possibly comprehend it and thinks, 'No way, that can't happen to me, I can't actually die.' Or like when you're little, the last couple of years when part of you knows Santa Claus isn't real, but the other part of you still believes in him. That's my theory, at least."

When we figured we'd gone about a mile and a half, we turned and headed back in the other direction. We changed the subject and talked some about school and people. Lately she'd been going out with Carter Escher, who was a senior and starting quarterback on our team.

"Who are you taking to the Soph-Phormal Dinner?" she asked.

"Nobody."

"You're not going?"

"Well, it's like you said, I care about dinner but I don't care about the Soph-Phormal Dinner."

"You have no school spirit," she said. "At least Aidan's on the marching band. Why don't you ask somebody? There are plenty of girls who'd like to go with you."

"No," I said. "I've made up my mind I'm not even going to think about dating until I have my driver's license."

That night I decided to show some school spirit by going to the football game. It was a home game and the first one

I'd gone to all year. My parents were actually going out together that night, to a retirement party, and they gave me a ride to the stadium. I would get a ride home with Skeepbo after the game.

I sat in the predominantly sophomore section. I saw Skeepbo in his uniform, sitting with the band. I saw Annie sitting with Starr and Tippy and the Aztecan Beauty and a bunch of others. I cheered at all the right moments, such as when Carter Escher cranked an eighty-yard touchdown pass to Tyler Gregerson, who had outrun the entire secondary.

During halftime I cheered inwardly for Skeepbo and the marching band.

After the game Skeepbo changed into his street clothes, and we walked over to the hamburger place before calling his mom for a ride. He carried his band uniform in a bag. We sat there in the noisy place eating our hamburgers. I had something I wanted to talk to him about.

"Have you ever had a sex talk with your father?" I asked.

Skeepbo had a mouth full of hamburger, and he continued chewing, eyeing me guardedly. Then he took a long sip of Coke. I waited. He shook his head. "No. He talked about self-abuse once. I thought he was just giving me another lecture about eating too much and being fat. But a day or two later it dawned on me that he was actually talking about whacking off. Why?"

"I don't know," I said. "Just curious."

"What do you wanna know?" he said.

"Not much. I have a few loose ends to tie up."

"You can look all that stuff up on the Internet, you know."

"It's not so much the information," I said. "It's more the . . ."

"The what?"

I hesitated. "The talk," I said. "Just having the talk."

When Skeepbo's mom dropped me off at my house, I noticed a strange car parked in our driveway behind my dad's. Mom's car was still gone; she and Dad wouldn't be home till late. I knew whose car this was: Fritz's.

I felt a surge of anger toward my sister. I had never met Fritz—I'd only seen him a couple of times; he had one of those manicured trimmed beards that are like a chin strap. As far as I knew, he wasn't a slimeball or anything—but still, my sister needed some serious straightening out.

I entered quietly through the kitchen door. Without turning on the kitchen light, I tiptoed over to the living-room threshold. In the living room the TV was on, but the volume was turned way down.

They were on the couch. Their clothes were still on, thank God, but their mouths were running amok over each other's faces. My sister was rubbing Fritz's groomed beard with her hands. Fritz's hands were groping all over her turd-brown Pizza Corner uniform. The sight of it gave me the same repulsed feeling as one of my sister's unflushed toilets.

I went back into the kitchen, flipped on the light,

coughed, whistled, opened the refrigerator, the cupboards, rattled the silverware drawer. I could almost hear the sucking sound of their lips pulling apart.

I grabbed a couple of cookies and went into the living room. A lamp had been turned on. Fritz and Lacy were sitting up straight, absorbed in a TV program.

"Gardner! How was the game? I don't think you've formally met Fritz."

"Hi, Gardner." Fritz stood up, smoothing his hair with his hand. "I've heard a lot about you." He extended his hand. I put my cookies on the coffee table, wiped my hand on my pants, and shook his.

"Whoa, your hand is cold," Fritz said. "Colder than a witch's you-know-what out there, huh?"

I could barely look at his face, knowing that his mouth had been racing all over my sister's face, and that his beard was probably sticky with her dried saliva.

"What are you watching?" I said.

"Some rerun," Fritz said. "Well, I'd better be goin'. Hey. Gardner. Great to finally meet you."

I gave him a nod. Lacy walked him to his car. I sat on the couch. Five minutes later, after the Miata had fired up and zoomed off, Lacy came back in.

"You're crazy," I told her. "You've gone off the deep end."

"Are you lecturing me, little brother?"

"Somebody's gotta step up to the plate and remind you you're eighteen and this guy's your twenty-eight-year-old boss. You're going to be really sorry when the thin ice you're skating on caves in."

I waited for her to laugh in my face, but she didn't.

In fact she smiled, not with derision but with admiration. Her whole face seemed to soften, and she looked pretty in the dim glow of the single lamp.

"Wow," she said. "You're growing up. You're actually able to see beyond yourself. It's cute."

"I'm the one giving the lecture here, not you," I said.

"How come you're such a prude? You saw us kissing, I take it."

"You call that kissing? I'll never be able to sit on that couch again."

"Oh, please." She closed her eyes.

"Now I know why you've been hiding your diary lately," I said.

She still had her eyes shut. "What I just said about you growing up? I take it back."

"You're going to get burned, you know that," I said.

"I'm going to bed." She headed for the stairs. "And I'm going to sleep till noon."

"I'm not done lecturing you."

She stopped at the foot of the stairs and turned around. "Hey, Gardner?"

"What?"

"Have you ever been with a girl?"

"What?"

"Have you ever made out with a girl on a couch?"

"What? Jeez—"

"Because if you have, then you know it won't do any good to lecture me. And if you haven't, then you're the one who needs the lecture, not me. Good night."

She floated up the stairs.

## 20

On the Sunday before Thanksgiving, Mom gave us all some shocking news: We weren't having Thanksgiving. At least not at our house. We were going to the Roydens'. Amy Royden was one of Mom's closest friends, a fellow girls' club member.

Of course, we'd been going over to Roydens' for get-togethers, barbecues, and parties from time immemorial. But that wasn't the same as spending Thanksgiving Day over there. It wasn't as though they were our relatives or anything.

I was surprised to see Dad's and Lacy's reaction. Dad only grumbled a little, and Lacy just shrugged.

Thanksgiving week it rained four inches in Seattle. Thanksgiving Day was wet and blustery, but the temperature was mild. We took Mom's car, which had always been our family car because it was bigger, cleaner, and better taken care of.

Dad asked Lacy to drive, but she didn't want to, so Dad got behind the wheel. I realized this was the first time the four of us had driven somewhere together since Dad's birthday.

While I had a captive audience, I thought it might be a good time to remind everybody that we still needed to reserve cabin number eight for July. But Dad started talking.

"We're not staying long," he said. "We're just going to eat the damn turkey and get the hell out."

"What's your hurry?" Mom said.

"The Roydens. The Roydens are my hurry. I don't like the Roydens, and I don't particularly care to hear them brag about how much money they have and how their kids are more advanced and gifted than anyone else's kids."

"Gee, that's a strange reversal," Mom said. "I thought that was my hang-up. I thought you were the one who didn't care about how rich everyone else is compared to us. As long as we're happy and everything, what difference does material wealth make, right?"

"I just don't like people who use their children as a way to show off. Trophy children."

Lacy, sitting to my right, heaved a big sigh. "You two aren't planning to squabble the whole way there, are you?

Because if you're planning to squabble the whole way there, maybe you can drop me off and I'll take Dad's car and meet you at the Roydens'."

"Oh, just zip it," Mom said. "I'll thank you not to use that snotty tone of voice, young lady."

"Don't 'young lady' me. I'm not ten years old."

"You sound like you are. You sound just like one of those snotty mall brats bitching at her mother."

"It's you and Dad who do all the bitching," Lacy said.

"That's enough. I said zip it."

"Since when am I not allowed to speak my mind?"

Mom looked out the window. "Now is not the time to talk about what you are and aren't allowed to 'get away with,' my dear."

We drove on in silence.

"I think I'll get drunk," Dad said, as if the idea had suddenly hit him. "That's it. That's how I'll get along with the Roydens."

"There are going to be two other couples besides the Roydens, Cam. The Donaldsons and the Pates."

"Now I know I'm going to get drunk."

"Don't talk that way. You're being a bad influence."

"Be prepared to drive home, because I'll be so snoggered, I won't even be able to tie my shoelaces. I'm going to watch football and drink myself into snoggerdom."

To my astonishment, Mom burst out laughing. It was genuine laughter. It seemed to ease the tension all around. Dad started laughing, too. So did I. Lacy, holding up a pocket mirror and applying makeup, didn't even crack a smile, though. I wondered what her problem was. Must be old Fritz. I thought she was wearing too much makeup. She looked hard, vampish. Not the old midwestern farm girl. She'd accuse me of being a prude, of course, which I suppose I was.

"I wouldn't trade our trophy kids for anyone else's," Dad said.

"Me neither," Mom said.

"I've got an idea," Dad said. "Let's bag this turkey dinner. Let's go get some pizza and take it to the park. We'll be the only ones there. We'll huddle under the shelter, watch the rain, eat pizza, and throw the Frisbee around. I didn't bring the Frisbee. We'll throw sticks around. Come on, let's do it. Let's be totally spontaneous."

"Don't be silly, Dad," Lacy said. "Nothing's open on Thanksgiving. Certainly not any pizza places."

"We'll do it another time, Cam," Mom said.

"Oh, yeah, sure we will," Dad said.

"All right, let's make a pact," Mom said. "Right here and now. Some Saturday or Sunday, when the weather's at least decent enough so we don't have to huddle under a shelter, we'll all get together, the four Dickinsons, and we'll go and get a pizza and take it to the park and do a picnic thing and throw the Frisbee around."

"All right," Dad said. "You heard it, kids. We've made a pact. You two are in on it. The Dickinson Frisbee Pact. No backing out, it is going to happen."

"Golly gee whiz," Lacy muttered, applying lipstick. "I can't wait."

We were almost to the Roydens'. Dad cleared his throat.

"Look, uh, there's something I've been wanting to say."

I saw Dad's hands tighten around the steering wheel. For some reason, my heartbeat accelerated and my stomach tightened.

"I've been doing a lot of thinking lately, in case you haven't noticed. I know I've been down in the dumps. First, I want to apologize to you all for my conduct these past weeks. For being so mired in my own selfishness. You've all been very patient with me, especially you, Jamie, and I'm thankful. I just want to say, starting Monday, I'm going to shift into high gear, start knocking on doors and making phone calls, get back in the game."

Mom turned to him. Her eyes were moist. "We all need some downtime every once in a while. Look, hon, we're at the end of November. We're coming into the holidays. There's no point in starting anything until the new year. My job's not going to taper off at least until March or April. It makes perfect sense for you to wait till January. New year, new start."

Dad nodded. I decided not to say anything about cabin number eight. We drove in silence, and for once it seemed to me a hopeful silence instead of a dreary one. But why had I got that feeling of dread?

The Roydens lived in a brick quasi-castle on a bluff in the Magnolia neighborhood of Seattle, overlooking Puget Sound. There were eighteen people at this turkey day gathering—four couples, assorted teenagers, and a pair of divorced aunts.

The main subject of conversation among the teenagers was skiing. I didn't mind it; the food was great and I stuffed myself.

Afterward not a single football game was turned on. Everybody just sat around the living room sipping after-dinner drinks and talking.

I went out for fresh air and a walk on the edge of the bluff. It was still raining and blustery. After a few minutes, Mr. Royden came out and stood under the covered gazebo and lit a cigar.

"Hey, Gardner, come over here a minute." He let out great puffs of cigar smoke; the smoke was the same color as his hair and neatly trimmed mustache. He wore a sweater and tie. Acting the squire of the great estate. I went over to him.

"I couldn't help noticing," he said, "you've been working out. You have bulked up in a big way. I'm wondering what equipment you've been using. Nautilus or what?"

"Actually, the ax," I said.

"Excuse me?"

"Chopping wood."

He laughed. "That's great. I spent four thousand bucks on a My-T-Gym, and you're hewing an ax. That's classic."

"I'm selling the firewood, too," I said, smiling. "You really have a My-T-Gym?"

"Downstairs. Go take a look at it later." He paused, took a couple of puffs. "Your old man still playing a lot of golf these days?"

"As much as November will let him," I said. "I think most of the courses are under water these days."

He chuckled. "I imagine he's got plenty of job prospects lined up."

My face burned. Why was Mr. Royden saying that? Was he being nosy or looking for a way to be helpful? Maybe he had tried to talk to Dad about it and Dad had snubbed him.

"Plenty," I said. "He's just kicking back until the new year."

Mr. Royden nodded.

Later, after another round of desserts, I wandered downstairs to see if I could find the My-T-Gym.

Passing by a big room that looked to be the library, I glanced in and saw Lacy. She was sitting in a wing chair reading a book, a glass of wine on the table next to her.

"Here you are," I said.

She looked up. "Here we are. The social outcasts. The great and glorious Dickinson children."

"Lifes of the party," I said.

"Displaying our multitude of talents," she said.

The walls were lined with books, and I scanned some of the titles. I saw Lacy take a sip of her wine. Her cheeks were flushed.

"What are you reading?" I asked her.

She shook her head and put the book aside. "Nothing. Just a book. About dog breeding, if you really want to know. Dog breeding is a fascinating subject, Gardner. There's a huge amount of importance placed on the breeding of dogs, the lineage, you know. Dogs, cats, horses."

"Hm. Sounds interesting."

"It is, actually. I mean, think of it. Breeding, genes, heredity, lineage. It's everything to animals—it determines their behavior, their disposition, their intelligence, abilities, and so on. But with people, breeding is downplayed in favor of other factors, such as environment, education, faith, willpower, that sort of thing. But my opinion is, I think breeding actually plays just as big a part with people as it does with dogs, cats, and horses."

"Why are we on this subject?" I said.

"Aren't you kind of curious to know why we—you and I—are so inferior to people like the Pates and Roydens and Donaldsons?"

"Excuse me?" I said.

"Oh, come on, Gardner. Look at the three Pate kids. They're gorgeous to look at, rich, bright, talented, witty. Now look at me. The best I can hope for is going to Bellingham next year. I'm plain, dull, and ordinary, and I work at a pizza joint. Is that my fault, or is it because of breeding? I think it's breeding. You can't fight heredity."

"Lacy, I've got news for you. One of you is worth ten of the Pates."

"That's nice of you to say, but impossible to support with evidence. Rich people are cute, and they breed with other cute people. Life is a beauty contest."

"You've been spending too much time under the pizza lamps," I said. "Or else that idiot Fritz has been teaching you this."

"Fritz isn't an idiot."

"Well, he is if he believes all that crap. Lacy, you know as well as I do, there's more to people than physical looks and how much money they have. That's so obvious, I shouldn't even have to say it."

"That's just Dad talking," she said almost giddily. "You learned it from Dad."

"So did you. And he's right."

"Oh, yes, he's so spiritual, isn't he? Well, look at where his spirituality has gotten him. He's a failure."

The word sounded so harsh and ugly coming from her. I shook my head slowly. "No, he isn't. He'll get it together in January."

"Right. And then we'll all go river rafting in Costa Rica."

"Why do you hate yourself so much?" I said.

"I'm just not in denial like you are. I've accepted who I am. People like you and me, people like the Dickinsons, we're not meant to be hotshots. We're not meant for greatness. You're going to hit smack up against that wall soon enough. The wall of breeding and heredity. The wall of limitation. The world is going to put you in your true place. You can thank our parents for that, and our grandparents, and great-grandparents. It's our ancestors who've saddled us with who we are, and we can never escape that. You are so much like Dad it's scary sometimes. And it ought to scare you. Stop fooling yourself."

She drained the rest of her wineglass in one gulp.

I left her sitting there with her empty glass. As far as I was concerned, I never wanted to look at her again.

## 21

Dad kicked back and waited for the new year. But in January he didn't shift into high gear or start knocking on doors. He just stayed home, adrift.

Part of me was worried about him—really worried. I thought it wasn't impossible that he could crack up and decide to blow his brains out, maybe even take us with him. I'd been noticing more of that in the news lately, grim stuff. A father going on a murder-suicide rampage. Another father killing his wife and kids with a hammer while they slept. Another father taking his son snowshoeing up in the woods and jumping off a ravine into a river, leaving the kid to wander around lost until he finally died of exposure. Who could say how close Dad was to the brink?

Another part of me was disgusted with my dad for not

doing anything. I wanted to grab him and yell in his face to snap out of it.

And I was disgusted with myself, too, for not trying to find more ways to help Dad. I had been too wrapped up in my own life.

In early February I heard Mom say to Dad: "It'll be a year in March. You're going to have to make a decision one of these days." She said it in a flat, tired voice, as if she didn't really care what he did. As if the life and love had gone out of her.

Yet I didn't believe she'd given up on him. Sometimes I'd see her look at Dad with that light in her eyes, or I'd hear her say something to him and laugh, and I knew she still loved him.

I still wanted to believe in Dad, too, enough to think he'd pull out of whatever he was going through and come to his senses.

The third week of February, each individual tenth-grade PE class was required to run the sixteen-hundred-meter race for time. My period's day came on Wednesday morning.

We jogged up the grassy hill to the red synthetic track. The temperature was in the low fifties, and the day was cloudy, with a fine, damp mist. The woods that rimmed the green playing fields were black against the gray sky, the tips of the trees hidden in mist.

Mr. LeGrand, our PE teacher, wearing shorts and T-shirt,

clipboard in hand and stopwatch on a black string dangling from around his neck, took roll while we did our stretching. He was a serious bodybuilder, and because he was on the short side, his muscles were stacked on top of each other with no place to go, giving him almost no flexibility. He had a flat-top crew cut and a high-pitched voice, and an even higher-pitched, good-hearted laugh.

When he finished taking roll, LeGrand noticed something on the far upper field, where the soccer team practiced. Slapping his clipboard against the top of one hairy thigh, he said, "Well I'll be a son of a trout farmer. There's that golfer again. I had to shoo him off a few days ago."

Mr. LeGrand didn't seem angry, just amused and slightly annoyed. I followed his line of vision and spotted a man hitting golf balls toward one of the soccer goals.

The man was dressed not like a golfer but like a bum, wearing an untucked baseball jersey and baggy maroon sweats with gaping holes in both knees. I knew the man and yet he was a stranger to me. He was my father.

Shaking his head, Mr. LeGrand said, "You guys keep doing your stretching while I go chase old Arnold Palmer away."

Mr. LeGrand started jogging out to the shabby golfer.

"I hope LeGrand pops him one," Janesco said, chuckling.

"Why do you hope that?" someone asked.

"I don't know. It'd just be cool to see LeGrand pop somebody."

I bent over and looked at the grass, concentrating on the

pull and stretch of my tendons. The grass blades had tiny beads of water on them. I filled my lungs with the morning air and tried to put my mind somewhere else. I tried to think of anything, the book I was currently reading, but I drew a blank.

Skeepbo came over to me and nudged me. "That your dad up there?" he muttered.

"Let's not advertise it."

"I hear ya."

I had never in my entire life felt anything but pride and admiration for my father. He had always been my number-one person in the world.

I straightened up from my stretching and looked across the field.

Mr. LeGrand was having what appeared to be an amiable conversation with Dad, who was leaning casually on his golf club and nodding. LeGrand said something, Dad said something back, both men laughed. LeGrand gestured toward us, his class. Dad nodded. The two men shook hands. A minute later LeGrand dropped his clipboard on the ground and assumed a golfing stance and was going into a slow-motion backswing with an imaginary golf club. Dad came around behind him and stood, as if they were having a romantic moment, guiding and adjusting Mr. LeGrand's short muscular arms, fussing with his grip. My classmates were all laughing.

"Coach is getting a free golf lesson from that guy," Tyler Gregerson said.

"Either that or it's a humping lesson," Janesco said. Everybody laughed.

At last, Mr. LeGrand looked at his watch, clapped his hands once, picked up his clipboard, and came running back to the group. My dad started collecting his golf balls, dropping them into a canvas bag.

"How we doing, gang?" LeGrand said when he reached us. "You men all stretched and limbered?"

"How was Arnie Palmer, coach?" Gregerson said.

"He give you a free cha-cha lesson?" Janesco said.

Mr. LeGrand joined in with the laughter. Then he looked at me, gave me a wink, and said, "Your old man says to smoke everybody in the sixteen hundred, Gardner."

All heads turned to me.

Then all heads turned to the man picking up golf balls.

Then back to me.

Silence fell on the group quicker than if someone had said "cancer."

I bent over and pulled up my socks. For a moment my embarrassment stung so bad, I thought I was going to have to run for the woods, just to escape the looks of all my classmates.

"Is that your dad?" Gregerson said.

"He's self-employed," I said.

"All right, let's line up for de sixteen hundred meters!" LeGrand said, slapping his clipboard again.

I found a place on the extreme outside. I didn't want to get tangled up in the crowd or boxed in on the first turn. I tried to calm myself, clear my thoughts, concentrate only on my breathing.

I looked over my shoulder to see if Dad was still there. He stood on the ridge of the hill above the track, watching.

He seemed far away.

Why had I said that to Gregerson? What a stupid, idiotic thing to say. Only someone who was ashamed and embarrassed for his father would feel the need to supply an excuse for him, and it would be obvious to Gregerson, Janesco, and the rest. They weren't stupid. They must have thought, "How pathetic that Gardner thought he needed to—"

LeGrand held up his arm.

"Everybody ready . . . ?"

Was I ashamed of my dad or of myself for giving up on him? Or was I ashamed for all those years I'd thought of him as a hero?

Had I given up on my dad? Had I finally accepted the fact that he was a failure and a bum and would stay that way?

"On your marks . . ."

All was quiet. I leaned in the starting position, my weight on my left foot, arms hanging loosely. I looked down at my fingers, waggled them.

"Get set . . ."

LeGrand kept his arm raised. It was so muscular that he couldn't even straighten it. I kept my eyes on the red synthetic track. My heart hammered.

"Go!"

I took off in an all-out sprint.

Down the straightaway, rounding the first curve, I pulled ahead of the thirty-some other runners. Still sprinting, I cut to the inside lane.

LeGrand's voice shrieked at my back: "DICKINSON! WHAT THE HELL DO YOU THINK YOU'RE DOING! YOU GOTTA PACE YOURSELF, OR YOU'RE GONNA DIE AFTER THE FIRST LAP! WHAT HAVE I TOLD YOU ABOUT PACING YOURSELF!"

I pushed even harder. As I finished the first lap, LeGrand called out my time and again screamed, "DICKINSON, WHAT ARE YOU DOING? YOU ARE GONNA DIE, MAN! WHAT ARE YOU DOING!?"

On the second lap, my head was hammering and my heart felt like it was going to burst. The pain was beyond excruciating, worse than anything I had experienced in all these months of running and chopping wood and lifting weights, but I kept pushing, kept my legs and arms pumping.

I was lapping stragglers as I finished the third lap. I passed Skeepbo, who was chugging along at his usual pace, more a fast walk than a run.

I no longer noticed the pain in my legs, because I couldn't breathe. All I could think about was my lungs and lack of breath. LeGrand shouted my time for the three laps and yelled, "KEEP IT UP! KEEP IT UP! KEEP IT UP! DON'T DIE! DON'T DIE!"

My sides were splitting, my throat sticking, my lungs and gut crumpling like a wadded sheet of paper. But my legs and arms kept pumping, my shoes pounded the track.

On the final stretch, I kicked with everything I had, thrusting my chest out, lifting my knees, forming fists with my hands. I crossed the finish line to the shouts and whoops of LeGrand. I staggered over to the grass, sucking air, fighting for breath. I doubled over and waited to see if I was going to live.

Finally I was able to walk and start to cool down. One by one, as my classmates finished the race, they came over to me and shook my hand, patted my back—Gregerson, Janesco, all the others. And at last Skeepbo.

And there was my dad, still there, watching from far off. Like a distant god, a million miles away, just watching.

Then he raised his fist high in the air.

## 22

"I sure was proud of you today, Gardner," Dad said that afternoon. He was in the garage amid all his stacks of magazines. "That's got to be the greatest race I've ever seen in my life, I mean it. You morphed on that final lap. Man, I've been walking on clouds all day. I'm glad I was there to see it. I hope I uh—didn't embarrass you."

"Embarrass me?"

"Your old man out there hitting golf balls at your school, in front of all your classmates."

"Oh . . . no."

"A little bit?"

I shrugged.

Dad nodded. "How's the firewood business going?"

"Not bad," I said.

"I might be able to throw a few customers your way. We could load up the car, and I could help you make the deliveries."

"All right," I said. "Thanks."

"I feel like it's been a while since we've really talked," Dad said. "That's been my fault."

"It's just the way things have been," I said.

"Yep, one of these days, we'll have to get away from here and go on an outing."

I nodded and started to walk away. Then I stopped and took a deep breath.

"Yeah," I said. "The trouble is, we talk about it but we don't do anything about it."

Dad's eyes rested on mine a moment.

"True," Dad said.

We stood in the garage not saying anything.

Then he nodded. "All right. Let's get out of here. Saturday. What do you say we take off—spur of the moment—get up before dawn, drive on over to . . . somewhere, I don't know, we'll figure something out. The coast. How about Dungeness Spit? That's where we'll go. We'll do it. We'll hike all the way out to the end of the spit. Five miles. Stay overnight in a motel, have a good meal, a little conversation, come back Sunday. What do you say?"

"You mean it?"

"Absolutely."

"You won't back out?"

"Not a chance."

"Let's do it," I said.

When Dad woke me up Saturday at dawn, I could hear it raining outside.

We drove north on I-5 on our way to the ferry terminal in Edmonds. He was drinking coffee from his big silver thermos. His voice, the rain outside, the coffee smell inside, gave me a good feeling.

"I hereby declare us free and unencumbered," Dad said. "None of the usual household rules apply. We can spit, swear, pull over to the side of the road and pee. The only thing not allowed is bullshit and censorship. So where do we start? What'll we talk about first?"

"Are you addicted to coffee?" I asked.

"Yep. Any other questions?"

I thought for a minute. "Mom's got her girls' club. I pretty much know what they do when they get together. You've got your own friends you've known since high school and college. What do you do when you get together with them?"

"Have a few beers, talk about old times, play some poker. Couple of them are fairly regular golfing buddies."

"Did you used to smoke pot?" I asked.

"That's none of your business."

"I thought you invited my questions."

"I invite them and welcome them. But we're not going to play Truth or Dare about Dad's old hijinks and ancient personal history. I'm your father; I'm not running for president."

"It's part of who you are—it's your past."

"Not really. Who a person used to be is a lot different from who the person is now. In fact, sometimes when I think back on who I used to be, I don't even know that person."

"But it's still part of your history," I said. "It would be included in your biography."

"Maybe, maybe not. Some things aren't even relevant to a person's life. My biographer might simply choose not to include certain things because they're irrelevant."

"I'd say drug use would be relevant," I said.

"I repeat, I'm your father, not a presidential candidate. I admit I did some things I'm not proud of. Those are things my children don't need to know about."

"That means you don't want us to have a real picture of you," I said. "A complete picture. You don't want us to know you as well as your friends know you."

"That's right. If you knew me in the same way my friends know me, I wouldn't be your father. I don't think a son or daughter should have a complete warts-and-all picture of their parent. Maybe there are certain bubbles that should never be burst. Maybe the father serves a higher purpose by being a hero to his son, with a little mystery about him, rather than just one of the guys. Would you really want to know all those nasty little things about your dad? Of course, I realize I probably lost my hero status with you a long time ago—probably around the time you stopped believing in Santa Claus. But maybe it's better for the father to be an invention of the children."

"Is that what God is?" I asked.

Dad glanced at me. "An invention of His children? Hm. Interesting question. What do you think? What's your opinion?"

I almost told him, No, I want to hear *your* opinion, but I stopped.

"If God were imperfect," I said, "we might not want to know it."

"You mean we'd rather take Him on faith than know the truth about Him?" Dad said. "If we knew everything about God, His weaknesses and mistakes, then He wouldn't be God anymore, and we'd have nothing to believe in? That's an interesting theory. Is that what you believe?"

"How do I know what I believe?" I said. "You've never told me what to believe."

"Give me a refill," he said, handing me his coffee cup.

I unscrewed the thermos and poured coffee into his cup and put the cup in the cup holder on the dashboard. The Edmonds turnoff came up, and Dad took the exit and headed west on 205th.

"I think I'd rather know you as a real human being," I said.

"Really?"

"Yeah. In some ways, you're more of a . . . well, an example to me now than you were when I believed that you were a—when I believed in Santa Claus. I think it helps me to know you did a lot of dumb things when you were my age. If you were some god or superhero, I wouldn't have any connection with you."

"That's a good point," Dad said. "I'll have to think about that some more."

We drove in silence for a while. The rain came down steadily and the wipers squeaked.

"How about some good old-fashioned facts-of-life questions?" Dad said. "Got any of those?"

"Facts-of-life questions?"

"Yeah. Birds-and-bees stuff. Now's your chance. It's been a long time since we covered the basics. We must have some catching up to do in that department."

I smiled and looked at him. "Are you serious?"

"Absolutely." He kept his eyes on the road.

I hesitated. "I'm warning you. I'm pretty ignorant."

"That's okay. That's fine."

"I mean, I'm so ignorant, you'll probably laugh your head off."

"I won't laugh."

"I do have a question," I said.

"Good. What is it?"

"What does it mean to do it 'doggie style'?"

Dad frowned slightly. "Well, just like it sounds."

My face felt hot. I looked out the window. "I know how dogs do it, I've seen that. But for people, they can do it that way, too? Or is it pretty much the only way it can be done?"

"Intercourse? Yes, it's a variation on the more traditional way. I believe that way is what's called the missionary position. Face-to-face."

"So if you're basically, say, not wearing any clothes and you're kissing, then without too much effort you could . . . do the missionary position."

"Yes. It does take some deliberate effort, though. It can't just happen accidentally or unintentionally."

"So it can be done either way. One position isn't more natural than another."

"I don't know about 'natural.' But I think in Western tradition, the predominant position is face to face. That may not be true of other cultures, I'm not sure."

I nodded. "Well. That clears up a lot of things. Thanks."

"No problem. Got any other questions of that nature?"

"No, not really. Not right now."

The sound came into view, all gray and placid, and Dad took the road that bypasses downtown Edmonds and leads directly to the ferry terminal. Even though it was Saturday, we were so early that the traffic was still pretty light. We sat parked in one of the lanes of cars waiting to drive onto the next ferry.

Dad turned off the motor. The wipers stopped in midposition.

"How, uh—" He cleared his throat. "You haven't been seeing any girls in particular, have you?"

"No."

"I assume you asked me about positions and such because you were just generally interested, which is absolutely understandable, and not because you're actually planning to experiment, in the near future, with a real, live member of the opposite sex."

I smiled. I didn't feel as embarrassed as I probably should have. I said, "Maybe there are some things about the son it's better the father didn't know."

"Touché," Dad said.

I waited a few seconds before saying, "No, I don't have any plans like that."

"That's wise," Dad said. "Remember this: Fifteen-year-old girls are a helluva lot more sophisticated and mature than fifteen-year-old boys. When I was fifteen, most of the girls my age dated juniors and seniors. If I were you, I'd stay a kid as long as I could, I wouldn't be in any hurry to act like a grown-up. Which is really what sex is. It's not only assuming the missionary position, it's assuming the grown-up position. It's saying goodbye to childhood."

For some reason I thought of that poem I'd written about the bike with training wheels.

"Oh, by the way," Dad said, "please tell me we don't need to talk about condoms. You've covered condoms in school, haven't you?"

"Yeah, we've had all that," I said.

"You think you might turn out for track? Not to change the subject or anything."

"I'm thinking about it. It would be a lot of work. A lot of commitment."

"No question about that."

"I like running, but I don't know if it's my calling in life. But I think I'll turn out anyway."

Dad nodded and smiled. "I'm glad to hear you say that. I think Mom'll be excited, too."

"Yeah." I hesitated. "I don't want to butt in or anything, you know, maybe this is just between you and Mom. But it seems like there'd be less friction if you went back to work. I mean, I thought I'd ask you if you're ever planning on getting a job."

"Fair question."

Car engines were starting up. A ferry worker in an orange vest started waving the columns of cars onto the loading ramp.

"Let's talk about that when we get on the ferry," Dad said.

**23**

During the short ferry ride across Puget Sound to Kingston, we got out of the car and climbed the stairs to the passenger deck. Dad wanted me to get something to eat, but I said I wasn't hungry. "You haven't had any breakfast," he said, frowning.

"I had part of a bagel."

"You need to eat a good breakfast. It's the most important meal of the day."

"I'm not hungry."

"Look," Dad said, when we had sat down opposite each other next to a window. "About this job thing. Yeah, I've been dragging my feet. Friction between your mom and me, I accept full blame for that. But it's a little more complicated than how you're seeing it, Gardner. In your eyes, the solution to all our problems is for old Dad to jump back on the treadmill. It's just not that simple."

"That's how you see it?" I said. "Like being stuck on a treadmill?"

I hadn't meant to say it accusingly, but Dad clammed up. We looked out the window at the gray sky and gray water, and the kelp and seaweed that floated by, and the south end of Whidbey Island in the distance.

"Losing to me at chess," I said. "That was a big blow to you, wasn't it? Another nail in the coffin and all that."

"Oh, I suppose a small part of me felt that way. But most of me, hey, I was proud of you. Watching you run that race, that made me proud. Talking to you now, listening to you, seeing how much you've grown and matured. Being able to have an intelligent conversation with you. It's great. But I feel guilty, too."

"Why guilty?"

Dad leaned forward, elbows on knees. "I'll be honest with you. All this thinking I've been doing these past months, you know, reflecting on my life, I can't help wondering if I haven't let you down. You and Lacy. It's one more thing I seem to have screwed up at: being a father. I should have taught you more. You know, music and language and carpentry and art and poetry and religion and philosophy— I should have done more. I should've worked harder at teaching and motivating you guys."

"You did plenty," I said.

"You feel that way?"

"Yeah."

"You don't feel like I've let you down?"

"No. Actually, I've kind of been thinking you're the one who's disappointed in me," I said. "In how I've turned out."

"What?"

"Well, I haven't exactly given you too much to brag about with me."

"Oh, man," Dad said, leaning back and rubbing his face. Then he leaned forward again. "Listen to me. I'm not—I've never, ever been anything but proud of you and Lacy. I've bragged about both of you, to anybody who'll listen, since the day you were born."

I looked away. "You haven't let us down either."

Dad shook his head with a flash of irritation. "I've been in this mental hole. I'm a mental case."

"Why haven't you gone to see a—"

"Because I need to work it out myself, that's why. I've worked it out. I know how to climb out of the hole. I have to make a new start."

"No offense, but you've said that before, Dad. About going out there and knocking on doors."

Dad looked out the window, and I saw his lips press together, and I thought I must have hurt him. I saw his chest rise and fall with steady breathing. Then slowly he turned to me, and I could tell somehow that he was hurting, not from what I had said but from what he was going to say.

"I was thinking more along the lines of a new life," he said.

I stared at him.

"I didn't mean to spring it on you like this," he said. "I forgot—I forgot my own preaching, about how a father shouldn't tell all to his son. But it feels like we're a couple of friends just sitting here, just being ourselves, not doing the father-and-son thing. I forgot. It's selfish of me to lay it on you all of a sudden. If I move on—you know, try something new, kind of strike off on my own—it doesn't mean I'm going to walk out of your life forever. But—"

I shook my head. I felt something cold and sharp digging into my stomach. The cold crept up to my throat and face. "No way," I said. I sounded like I'd caught him trying to cheat at Monopoly. "No, you can't do that. You can't just quit on us and run off and start some new life." I laughed at the craziness and unfairness of it.

"I haven't said anything to your mom yet, Gardner. And I might not. Not face to face. I still love her, but I don't see the point in having some big ugly scene with her. I thought it would be better just to leave a simple note. I won't take any-thing—nothing but my car and a bag and my golf clubs. And some cash. I'll leave the checkbook and all the credit cards behind. I know it sounds crazy and cruel and selfish. But you and Lacy aren't little kids. Your mom can take care of herself."

I was having trouble breathing. "Why don't you—why can't you just take a long trip," I said. "Try going away for a month."

He shook his head. "You don't get it. I'm desperate."

I shook my head. I could feel tears coming to my eyes. I knew I wasn't going to cry, because they weren't those kind of tears; it was more like my eyes were burning.

"I know it's selfish," he said. "Hey, I've always believed in duty and self-sacrifice. I've always been critical of people who choose their own well-being over their family's. But Gardner, if I don't do this, I swear to God . . . it'll be worse than putting a gun to my head and blowing my brains out. It'll be a slow death. A giving up. Accepting that my life is a failure. I can't do that. This is the only life I've got, for Christ's sake. I'm forty-nine. I used to think life would go on forever, in some form. I thought God wouldn't let us just go out of existence. But I'm not going to sit around and wait to find out if there's a heaven or not. Dammit, I'm going to take what's left of my life and run with it. If I go down in flames, then so be it. I'm starting over. If that's against the rules, then screw the rules. There are no rules."

When the ferry docked at Kingston, we got back in the car and drove up Highway 101 until we reached the town of Sequim. Flat farmland stretched out toward the Strait of Juan de Fuca. The rain forest and the Olympic Mountains were to the south. We checked into a motel, then found a family restaurant and ate some lunch. Outside the rain fell steadily, not heavy but a dense, seeping rain-forest rain.

Back in the motel room, we changed into our rain gear and drove to Dungeness Recreation Area, where we parked the car near the campground. We started hiking down the muddy trail through the woods, on down to the beach. The rain was fine and very dense.

Dungeness Spit is a five-and-a-half-mile sand finger, the longest natural sand spit in the United States, jutting out into the Strait of Juan de Fuca. Tons of twisted and gnarled driftwood were piled up on the beach. Out near the tip of the spit was a lighthouse with its beacon blinking. Across the strait was Vancouver Island and Victoria.

Dad and I had never hiked the entire spit. After the first couple of miles, there wasn't another soul walking the spit, just us and seagulls and a dozen other kinds of waterfowl.

We hiked all the way out to the lighthouse. We sat down and ate a snack, then turned around and came back the other way.

We didn't talk much. I didn't feel good, but I couldn't hate my dad. Maybe I couldn't even blame him for wanting to escape us.

When we got back to the car, we went into the rest room and changed into dry clothes. It was getting to be evening. Back at the hotel, I tried to read a book while Dad took a shower, and he napped while I took mine. Then we went to a seafood restaurant in Sequim.

On his second beer, Dad grew more talkative, and he told me about how when he was my age, he would study the Bible and go to church and talk to God. He committed himself to spiritual growth. Even in college and after, he shunned material things. In the first few years in his job, when Lacy and I were very small, he waited for God's calling, although he stopped going to church. Gradually the whole idea of God kept getting more and more distant until finally God became nothing but a word, distant and far removed from material life, irrelevant.

That was a surprise to me. I had always thought Dad had a pretty solid faith in God. True, he had never given Lacy or me any direction in that department. But that was because, or so I had always thought, Dad figured if we wanted to find God bad enough, we'd seek Him out ourselves.

Then Dad told me something else I'd never heard before.

"When I was, oh, a couple years younger than you," he said, taking a sip of his beer, "I had this plan. I was going to run away from home, live off the land, be a hobo or drifter—or maybe a wandering monk. A pilgrim. You know, maybe work an odd job here and there, just to put money in my pocket. I planned and plotted. I didn't know when I'd do it, but I thought, 'one of these days.' I actually kept a backpack, packed with my traveling gear, all ready to grab on the spur of the moment and go. I kept it hidden way in the back of my closet."

"Didn't you get along with your parents?" I asked.

"No, no, it had nothing to do with that. I wasn't running *away* from anything. I didn't want to run off and join the circus or the Foreign Legion or anything. I just wanted to wander the world and have adventures and seek wisdom and set my soul free."

"You never did run away, though?"

"Never did. I did some traveling after college, before your mom and I got married, but that wasn't the same thing. That was more like an extended vacation, really. I never got that bug out of my system."

"You still have the backpack?" I asked.

"Hm?" He was looking away and hadn't seemed to hear me.

No, I didn't hate Dad, and I didn't even feel bitter toward him. I just felt sad for him. He seemed pathetic.

"So that's what you're going to do?" I said. "Roam around the rest of your life?"

"I don't know," Dad said. "I'd like to head south. Go down to Mexico."

"That's a real plan," I said.

He cut me a sharp look and took a long drink of beer. He looked like a kid. A lousy little kid. He hadn't grown up at all since the time he'd kept the backpack hidden away in his closet. He had spent his whole life not knowing what he wanted, not even knowing how to find it.

The one thing he had wanted to do—to run away—he'd never had the courage to go for it. That was the waste. That was the failure.

These past months, I'd been worried about my father becoming more distant, becoming a stranger to me. But I'd been wrong. My dad hadn't become a stranger. I had never really known him. For fifteen years he'd been my father and even my best friend and hero. We'd spent thousands of hours together, done all sorts of things. But I didn't know the man Camden Dickinson, and I probably never would.

In the morning we drove home. I didn't tell anyone about what my dad had said.

Track turnouts started the following week, and I showed up. To my surprise, so did Annie.

I would like to say that I finally found my calling in life. But I hated track.

The workouts were living hell—a long way from those leisurely runs on the Burke-Gilman Trail.

I griped and whined a few times to Annie, but she didn't give me much sympathy. She said she didn't mind the hard work. I considered quitting. Why waste my time on something that made me miserable?

But I stayed with it.

And so did Dad.

That's not to say I didn't wonder if one day I'd come home from track practice and find a goodbye note taped to the kitchen counter, and he'd be gone, and I wouldn't see him again until I was twenty-five.

Would I hate him if he did that? Would I quit running and give up on everything just to spite him? I didn't know. I was all confused. I didn't really think he would leave us. But why not? Was he staying because he lacked the guts to run? Or did it take more guts to stay and not run? And did I still believe that my dad had any guts at all? That was what I couldn't figure out.

## 24

On the first Sunday in March, I slept in till around ten. My body ached from the week's worth of torture.

When I finally dragged myself out of bed and stared out the window, I saw a glorious day that could have passed for spring. I forced myself to do some reps with the weight-lifting bar, then go out to the backyard and chop some wood. But my body didn't want any part of it. After I took my shower, I went downstairs and found my mom in the living room in the bright sunlight, drinking coffee and reading the Sunday paper. Dad had gone off to play golf. Lacy was still in bed.

I took a moment to actually look at my mom. I hadn't really looked at her for a long time. She had bags under her eyes, but she pretty much looked about the same as usual.

She glanced up from the paper.

"What's up?" she said.

"Nothing," I said. I didn't want her to think I'd been looking at her.

Suddenly, Dad came bursting into the house from out of nowhere and announced that he had canceled his golf game and was going to make the Dickinsons fulfill the promise they'd made on Thanksgiving. He ran around shouting, "The Dickinson Frisbee Pact! The Dickinson Frisbee Pact!"

Mom was laughing at him.

Dad rousted Lacy out of bed.

"Why don't I make some sandwiches or something more picnicky?" Mom said.

But Dad didn't want to be burdened with a bunch of picnic paraphernalia. "Put on your shoes, get in the car, and go," he said. "Before the phone rings. Before we have time to think about it and change our minds."

Mom hurried upstairs to get dressed. Lacy moaned and complained, but once she had put her makeup on, she seemed to perk up. She even said she didn't mind eating pizza on her pizza day off, so we got in Mom's car, Lacy behind the wheel, Dad in the front seat next to her, spinning the Frisbee in his lap, Mom and me in the back. After stopping at Pizza Corner for a pizza and six-pack of pop, we headed for one of our favorite secluded parks.

"I have to admit it's a gorgeous day," Lacy said. "Look at those"—she interrupted herself with a gaping yawn—"mountains."

"Late night?" I said.

She aimed a heavy-eyed glower at me in the rearview mirror.

The park was truly hidden. You had to leave the car in a gravel turnaround and walk about a hundred yards down a narrow path that cut through dense blackberry bushes, until it opened up into a grassy field with a picnic table. Nearby was a hill, on top of which was a gigantic swing set, along with one of the last remaining teeter-totters in the city of Seattle.

We left the pizza and six-pack on the picnic table and hiked up to the top of the hill to check out the view to the southwest, the hazy Seattle skyline twenty miles away. There were only two swings, so Mom and Dad snatched them, while Lacy and I stood together watching them as if we were the playground supervisors.

"They almost look happy," she said.

She and I were on shaky speaking terms, never having quite recovered from our little scene at the Roydens' on Thanksgiving. She had never apologized for what she'd said or even tried to follow it up with a rational explanation. I felt as though she'd taken a marking pen and drawn a big X across my face.

"Sorry about that crack I made in the car," I said.

"That's okay. Prude."

"How's Fritz?"

"Do you care?"

"Oh, always."

"He wants me to move in with him this summer. Just keep going to community college so we can be together."

"Good old Fritz. Always putting your interests ahead of his."

"You don't understand," she said. "He's begging me not to go to Bellingham next year. It's nice to be wanted."

"What did you tell him?"

"Summer's a long way off."

I could feel my stomach growling. I hadn't had any breakfast, and I was starving.

"Wanna do the teeter-totter before the city yanks it out for being unsafe?" I said.

"Sure. If I can trust you not to jump off while I'm in midair."

"I'm mean, but not that mean."

Just as we were climbing on, we were interrupted by a sharp, sudden cry from Mom, who had skidded to a stop and was pointing down the hill toward the picnic table.

Dad, too, put on the brakes. "Sweet mother of God," he said. "I do not even believe it."

Lacy and I turned to where Mom and Dad were looking. Our picnic table was swarming with crows. There were so many, I couldn't begin to count them. Somehow they had pushed aside the six-pack and pried open the lid of the pizza box and were on top of each other in a feeding frenzy, grabbing chunks of pizza and trying to escape from the crowpile, cawing, flapping, fighting like vultures.

All we could do was stand at the top of the hill and watch.

Lacy said, "This is one of those things you look back on and laugh about." She tried to laugh, but it sounded like a whimper.

We walked down the hill. The crows flew off one by one. The boldest stayed to stab at the last remaining scraps until nothing was left on the table but the six-pack and the cardboard box with its wax paper full of holes from where the crows had pecked at it.

25

A couple of Sunday evenings after that, Dad rounded us up and said he had something to tell us. I got that sick feeling in my stomach.

Lacy and I sat on the couch, Mom in one of the chairs. Dad paced back and forth in front of the TV.

"About three weeks ago, I called Jeff Royden. As you probably know, he spends a large portion of his life playing golf and schmoozing with corporate big shots. He said he'd be glad to say a few words on my behalf to one of his golfing cronies, who happens to be the vice president of a start-up Internet dot-com company. This VP talked to his personnel department, who in turn invited me to come and interview for a couple of different positions. Last week, while no one was looking, I dug out my suit and tie and drove on over to Redmond for what is called a . . . uh . . ." Dad hesitated and scratched his head.

"First-round interview?" Mom said.

"Close enough. They put me through about five interviews in three hours, and everybody seemed to like me well enough, and I thought one particular job in marketing sounded somewhat interesting. The salary's negotiable, of course, but it'll be decent, trust me on that. So the upshot is, I have to go back day after tomorrow for a final interview. I won't go so far as to say it's a done deal, but the interview is mainly just to talk with the department head, who is a twenty-four-year-old snot who also happens to play golf with that same VP who plays golf with Royden. So assuming we're compatible, most likely they'll offer me the job."

"I don't believe it," Mom said, her mouth hanging open. "Cam. I don't believe it."

"You don't sound too happy," Dad said. "Which part don't you believe? The twenty-four-year-old department head?"

"I—I'm ecstatic. I just can't believe you called Jeff Royden."

"It was relatively painless," Dad said. "The crows ate our pizza, I got back at them by eating crow."

It got a laugh from me.

"So you think you're going to take it?" Mom said. "You think it's something you'd like to do? You have the skills they want?"

Dad nodded. "Yeah."

"And it's where? Redmond? You wouldn't mind commuting all the way over there every day?"

"It'll give me a chance to try some of those books on tape."

"What's the company like?"

"Office park. Duck pond. Wooded trails. Techies half my age walking around in Birkenstocks and Levi's."

"And you think the salary will be . . . ?"

"More than enough for you to quit working."

"Cam, aren't you excited?"

Dad nodded again. There he stood, in front of the TV, nodding, and to me he looked deflated and lost.

Tuesday morning I sat at the kitchen table eating toast and cereal, watching the rain hammering the flowers and shrubs in our backyard. Dad came down all duded up and shaved and groomed. It was only about the third time in my life I'd seen him wearing a suit and tie. Mom followed him a minute later, kissed him, wished him luck, and took off for work, as she had some early appointments. Next came Lacy. She grabbed a muffin, kissed Dad on the cheek, and was gone.

Dad, frowning, watched me eat for a while. "You want a ride to the bus stop?"

"No, that's okay. It's only a five-minute walk."

"It's pouring down rain out there."

"I don't mind."

"When do you have to leave?"

"For the bus? Not for another twenty minutes."

"How's track?"

"I'm hanging in there. I only wake up screaming every other night now."

Dad chuckled, jingled his car keys in his pocket. "Aidan turns sixteen next week, doesn't he?"

"Yep. A week from tomorrow."

"He's still hoping for a truck?"

"I'd say it's a sure thing. But I could be wrong."

Dad filled his thermos with coffee and switched off the coffeemaker.

"Well," he said, "I'm way early, but I think I'll hit the road. You never know about that bridge traffic."

"Smoke 'em in that interview," I said.

"Thanks. You don't mind staying here by yourself?"

"I don't think it'll scar me for life."

He smiled. "When do you leave for your bus?"

"In about nineteen minutes now."

"Did you eat a good breakfast?"

"You're seeing me do it."

"Breakfast is the most important meal of the day." He smiled. "I guess you haven't heard that before."

Holding his thermos in one hand, he picked up his briefcase, the one Lacy had given him for his birthday. "Well . . . I'll see you, Gardner."

"Good luck," I said.

"I'm a little nervous," he said. "I couldn't eat any breakfast. Call me a hypocrite."

"You'll knock 'em dead."

"Gardner . . ."

"Yeah?"

"You know, I—I've been meaning to . . . Well, thanks, for not saying anything to your mom . . . you know . . . about what I said to you. Thanks for keeping quiet about all that between you and me."

"Sure."

"You helped straighten me out."

"I didn't do anything."

"Just talking to you, you know, that really helped me screw my head on."

I nodded. "Yeah."

"I'm going to watch some of your track meets this spring," he said.

"I'm not on varsity," I said. "Competition for the sixteen hundred is pretty fierce. There are plenty of juniors and seniors to fill the slots."

"Oh, well, that's all right. Nothing wrong with being on JV. You'll make varsity next year."

He waved and went out through the kitchen door. I heard his car start up and drive away.

I sat in the kitchen. Five minutes passed. I just stayed at the table, staring out at the backyard and the rain.

Something didn't seem right. I should have been more excited for Dad.

I got up and put my dishes in the dishwasher, then went and brushed my teeth. The minutes went by slowly. I knew

I should gather up my stuff and leave for the bus stop, but I went back to the kitchen and sat at the table and tried to figure out what was bothering me.

I felt as though I should have said something more to Dad, but I didn't know what.

When I looked at the clock, I saw that somehow another ten minutes had passed. I wouldn't make the bus now. It didn't matter. I'd walk to school, get drenched, be a few minutes late. Or maybe I wouldn't even go to school. Maybe I'd play hooky, sit home and read all day. Gee whiz, that unexcused absence on my record might haunt me for the rest of my days, keep me from running for—

The front door burst open.

"Gardner?"

It was Dad.

"Gardner!"

"In here. In the kitchen."

I heard his heavy footsteps.

"How come you're still here?" he asked.

"I, uh—"

"Oh, never mind. Hey, pardner, I got trouble."

He explained that his car was a half mile away on the highway shoulder with a flat tire. He had slogged back to the house to put on some old clothes so he could change the tire; he didn't have time to wait for Triple A to show up. But now since I was still here . . .

He opened his umbrella, and we hurried along the sidewalk. The rain bounced off the cement, filling the gutters. It was strange to be walking down the sidewalk with my dad. Such an ordinary thing to do, really, walk down a sidewalk, but not something you do with your father.

"Wouldn't you know something like this would happen," Dad said.

"Maybe it's a sign," I said.

"What?"

"Maybe it's a sign. A warning."

Dad didn't say anything for a few paces. "No such thing as signs or warnings," he said at last. "Besides, I don't know what you're talking about."

"Yes, you do," I said.

He said nothing.

We walked two more blocks and reached the busy highway. There was no sidewalk here. We had to edge along the shoulder for about three hundred yards. A nonstop stream of traffic swept past us at an uncomfortably high speed. I couldn't imagine it, every morning and evening, five days a week, being stuck in this.

Dad had to use his umbrella to shield himself not only from the rain but from the splashing of passing cars. He also had to step around the muddy spots as best he could. I didn't wait for him to keep up with me; he had given me his keys, so I hurried on ahead to his car.

The good news was that the flat was on the right rear side, away from the traffic. The bad news was that the drainage here was terrible: Dad had brought the car to a stop in three inches of standing water.

I opened the trunk. You had to lift the bottom panel to get the spare and jack out. Trouble was, I couldn't get at the floor panel because the trunk was full of Dad's crap. I had to take out two boxes full of magazines—I couldn't tell whether he was getting rid of them or adding them to his hoard in the garage. I put them on the pavement, where they immediately started to get soaked, but I didn't give a rip. His golf bag was in there, too, so I just shoved it over to the far side of the trunk.

It struck me as strange that he would keep his clubs in his trunk. These Toyota trunks were easy to break into; I'd be worried about somebody stealing my clubs. Could be he'd forgotten to take them out after his last golf game. Or maybe he planned to hit the driving range after his interview.

I noticed something else. Stuffed way back inside the trunk, I saw a hiker's backpack, bulging, obviously packed full.

I had to get moving. I lifted the panel, took out all the tire-changing equipment and the temporary spare tire, and waded into the pond to start loosening the lug nuts.

By then Dad had reached the car, and he stood by giving me occasional directions, also trying to keep himself from getting splattered with mud or water, while I grappled with the jack and lug nuts and spare and all the minor hassles of changing a tire. Fifteen minutes later, soaked completely to the skin, I raised my hands in victory.

"Done."

"You did it. Hey, Gardner—"

"You better get going, Dad."

He had to raise his voice to be heard above the rain, the traffic, and the splashing of tires. "Get in, let me drive you home so you can change."

"You don't have time for that," I said. "Look, I can't get any wetter. You can't turn around here. You'd have to drive up the highway for miles before you could even make a U-turn. Then you'd have to drive me all the way back home, drop me off, then turn right around and go through this traffic again. And it's getting thicker. Just get going. You're losing time. I'll walk back and change clothes. Then I'll walk to school."

"Gardner—"

"Just go, Dad."

"Wait, I'll write you a note."

He went into his car, found a scrap of paper, and scribbled a tardy note. While he was doing that, I opened the trunk and screwed everything back in place as best I could, replaced the panel, and loaded the two soggy boxes of magazines in last. Before I closed the trunk, I took another long look at the backpack.

When I looked up, I noticed Dad standing beside me, watching me, holding his umbrella and the scrap of paper. I straightened up and slammed the trunk closed.

He stuck out his right hand to shake. "I owe you one, pard."

I held up my hands. "Don't touch me. I'm filthy."

He nodded. Our eyes met.

"Gardner . . ."

"Go."

He didn't move. His eyes traveled over to the trunk. He seemed to want to say something. Every inch of me was soaking wet. I looked up at his face.

"Just drive," I said. "Go to Mexico. Now's your chance. Run away. You're miserable. I don't want to see you like that. I'd rather have you split than see you be miserable. I won't hate you for leaving. I won't hate you. If you're staying because you don't want to let me down, don't do it. You said it would be a slow death, staying here. You said that. You told me you were going to leave, now do it. For once in your life, do what you say you're going to do. Don't just roll over. Run! Start over. Start a new life."

He stood there with his mouth open, just staring into my face, his eyes wide and startled. Then he seemed to snap out of it and remember the note he was holding. He thrust it out to me. The paper was dry because he'd held it under the umbrella, but I was so wet I had nowhere to put it, so I stuffed it down inside my underpants.

Finally, Dad turned and got back into his car. I watched him start it up and wait for someone to let him in, then ease his way out into the heavy stream of traffic and accelerate, the water flying up behind his rear tires in a rooster tail. Brake lights of all the cars in his lane came on in a chain reaction, the cars slowed, then the red lights went off again and they sped up. They looked like a herd of animals. Each one no different from the rest. I stood there another minute or two. Long after Dad's car had rounded the bend and disappeared, I watched the traffic, the endless stream of cars.

## 26

That day at school was agony. Not so much because I wondered whether I'd ever see him again, but because I was torn in half between wanting him to be there when I got home and wanting him to be gone.

When I got home that evening, his car was in the driveway, and Dad was in the kitchen fixing dinner.

They offered him the job a few days later, and he accepted it.

He's been there a month now. He's removed the two boxes of magazines from his trunk, but his golf clubs and backpack are still there. I know because I've checked. Twice.

Sometimes he seems happy and he jokes around; more often he just seems to be going through the motions.

Lacy hasn't decided what she's going to do. Fritz still

wants her to move in with him and stay put in community college.

Skeepbo's parents went all out for his birthday. They hired a limo to take the two of us to the Space Needle for dinner. Afterward we walked back to the loading zone where we'd arranged to meet the limo, only there was no limo. In its place was a brand-new Ford Ranger pickup truck. Dark blue. The limo driver handed Skeepbo the keys and said, "Happy birthday from your parents. Please drive carefully."

The poor abused kid.

Now I don't have to take the bus to school. Skeepbo comes by and picks me up. Sometimes at night Skeepbo and I go driving around and talk about the past, present, and future and stop for hamburgers. He's starting to get the hang of handling a truck and eating a hamburger at the same time.

His parents are on him now about going to that fat farm again this summer. They're also pushing him to go to Ambalm Prep next fall. He's told them the fat farm, maybe, but Ambalm Prep, forget it, no way. But I say hey, why not? You can't just ignore an opportunity like that. Latin, fencing, lacrosse, reenactments of historical battles—a great opportunity. A chance to start a new life, really challenge and push yourself to your limit and beyond.

Skeepbo wants to know how much his parents are paying me to say that.

My mom hasn't quit her job yet. Maybe she doesn't trust my dad, sees that he's still restless and moody, senses that one day he will bolt. She has sworn a sacred oath that on the first weekend in June, she is having a garage sale. She's circled the date, it's written in stone. Even Dad realizes that she's serious, so he's been boxing some of the stuff he absolutely can't bear to part with and labeling it with a NOT FOR SALE sticker. Lacy and I are looking forward to the garage sale. We've always thought Dad's assortment of oddities would attract some pretty interesting characters, and now we'll find out.

There won't be any vacation at the beach this summer, no cabin number eight. Everybody will be working, including me, as I'm now old enough to get a work permit and a part-time job. I tell Skeepbo we ought to get a paper route together. Think of it, I tell him. We'd use your truck. You sit there and drive, I run from house to house tossing papers. Great exercise for both of us. He thinks I'm joking. But I can think of a lot worse jobs than delivering newspapers for a couple of hours in the morning.

Annie recently got her driver's license, but she has only occasional access to a car. She made varsity, I'm on JV. Now that the meets have started, the workouts aren't so bad. I know that track isn't my life's passion, but I feel kind of proud of myself for staying with it and not bailing out.

We're still friends, Annie and me, and there's still a long line of guys wanting to go out with her, and I guess I'm somewhere in that line.

Skeepbo and I will probably always be friends.

And the Dickinsons, we're still together. Nobody's bailed out yet. As for what might happen one of these days, who knows. I'm not going to worry about it. I'm through sitting around waiting for life to happen. Like Dad said, I'll take what's left of my life and run with it.

Lacy said that if our family were a sitcom, the show could be called *Here Come the Dickinsons.* How about just *Here Are the Dickinsons.* For now. Go, Dickinsons. Long may you run.